SASQUATCH - LEGEND IN THE SHADOWS

Mark A. Wilson

PublishAmerica
Baltimore

© 2010 by Mark A. Wilson.
All rights reserved. No part of this book may be reproduced, stored in a retrieval system or transmitted in any form or by any means without the prior written permission of the publishers, except by a reviewer who may quote brief passages in a review to be printed in a newspaper, magazine or journal.

First printing

All characters in this book are fictitious, and any resemblance to real persons, living or dead, is coincidental.

PublishAmerica has allowed this work to remain exactly as the author intended, verbatim, without editorial input.

Hardcover 978-1-4512-4852-4
Softcover 978-1-4512-4853-1
PUBLISHED BY PUBLISHAMERICA, LLLP
www.publishamerica.com
Baltimore

Printed in the United States of America

DEDICATIONS

*To my two young nephews
Ethan Miller and Chase Watkins
And to their great Grandmother, Eleanor Raine for doing a
fantastic job of proofreading.*

ACKNOWLEDGEMENT

To my wife Brenda Kay, without whose guidance I would be lost.

*Previous Books Written By
Mark A. Wilson*

THE AMAZING GIFT FROM THE WOODS
THE LEGEND OF CRAWLEY CREEK
CURSE OF THE LOST JOURNAL
THE OLD MAN'S SECRET FRIEND
THE SECRET OF GRAY VIEW MANOR
THE DEMONS WITHIN

TABLE OF CONTENTS

PRELUDE 11
CHAPTER 1 13
CHAPTER 2 26
CHAPTER 3 48
CHAPTER 4 85
CHAPTER 5 89
CHAPTER 6 94
CHAPTER 7 97
CHAPTER 8 107
CHAPTER 9 112
CHAPTER 10 124
CHAPTER 11 137
CHAPTER 12 154
CHAPTER 13 168

PRELUDE

With the glowing red eyes of the beast cast upon him, Ethan was now so scared that he was unable to move. The huge hairy creature began a slow advance towards the helpless young man. Paralyzed with fear and believing death was only moments away, Ethan closed his eyes tightly. As the sweat began to run down his face, Ethan desperately wanted to run away. As the creature got closer and closer, it never once took its eyes off its victim. The thought of this monster, this living nightmare biting into his flesh was too much to comprehend. He could soon feel its hot breath now on his face and a terrible odor filled the air. Cringing and beginning to shake uncontrollably, he knew his life was over.

CHAPTER 1

It has been quite a good year so far, for young Ethan Miller. During his senior year in high school, he has made the honor roll, and is a star on the baseball team. His days are happy and busy, but it is the nights that trouble him. He is having a recurring and persistent dream about a large hairy beast that walks on two legs coming after him. He awakens with a fright from this vision in the middle of the night, completely out of breath and covered in a cold sweat. Confused and baffled at what it means, he tries very hard to put it off as nonsense; however, the dreams persist. They are getting more vivid and real, and they now include Native Americans. Ethan is not sure if he should tell anyone about these dreams; his friends may think he is losing his mind. After thinking about it carefully, he has decided that for now he will keep these annoying dreams to himself. He is hoping that his overactive imagination will soon subside, these crazy visions will be gone, and he can concentrate on college. However, the very next day, he by chance glances over and looks into a bookstore window while walking down the street. Noticing something familiar, he instantly stops to get a better look, young Ethan is surprised and shocked by what he sees. Spellbound, he needs a minute to catch his breath and rub his eyes. Now pressing his face right up to the glass, his mouth drops open, he is speechless. There in the display case he sees the vision from his dreams on the cover of a book. This cover shows a hairy beast standing on two legs at the edge of a forest, and a man is in the foreground next to a totem pole. Intrigued and needing to learn more, he can see the title, (Mystery Of The Shadow Beast). Ethan has a strange feeling at this point, and he asks himself, "Is this just a coincidence, or does it mean much more?"

Young Ethan stares longingly at the image, and every detail and feature is exactly like those in his dreams. Ethan has never believed in spirits or the supernatural, and he certainly doesn't believe in premonitions.

Scratching his head and looking at this book cover, he had to admit, that this was very unusual. Glancing at the bottom of the book, he finds the author's name, (M.A. Wilson). Thinking for a second if he has ever heard of this person, the name does sound familiar to him.

It suddenly becomes eerily quiet; and the sounds of the city can no longer be heard. Mesmerized at this point, he feels himself being drawn into the image. The ground vibrates from a single drum beat, boom…boom…boom.

Smoke from a campfire fills his nostrils, and a slight wind blows his hair to one side. Fleeting images now flash before his eyes, strange images that cause him to shiver and make his skin grow cold.

Ethan is beginning to breathe heavier now, and the brief images show Indians, a mother elk, her calf and then the face of a large creature. This last image causes him to step back. Very confused and puzzled, he reaches down and rubs his right leg as a sharp pain shoots from his hip to his ankle. As he is about to go inside the bookstore and investigate further, however, at this moment, he snaps out of his trance when he hears the sound of a car horn. Turning around, he can see a group of his friends hanging out a car window. They call to him, "Hey, Ethan, meet us at the swimming pool."

Without thinking twice, Ethan now hurries down the street to catch up to them. The swimming pool is where all the kids hung out, and it was a popular place to meet girls. His troubled dreams about the hairy beast and finding this strange book cover are soon forgotten and are out of his thoughts.

During the next two months, he works as much as he can to save up money for college. His unusual dreams seemed to have vanished, and he now prepares to move away from home.

The rest of the summer has passed by so fast that before he realizes it, he is enrolled at Oregon State University and living in the dorm. It takes several weeks for him to get adjusted to college life and living with so many other people.

His classes are hectic and frenzied, but he is still doing well in his studies. It is his first extended trip away from home and he misses his family back in Wisconsin very much, and at times is home sick. The letters he receives from home, along with an occasional package containing his favorite cookies always makes him feel better. However, Ethan knew even before graduating from high school what he wanted to do with the rest of his life. His mind was firmly made up the year before graduating high school: he wanted to pursue a career in teaching. He selected Oregon State University because of its excellent academic programs, up to date facilities, and most importantly its location. He had always wanted to explore the vast wilderness of the Pacific Northwest, and this was his chance to do so. He knew he would be far from home, but he also knew that four-years would go by quickly. Besides, he told his parents that he would come home for Christmas and spring break.

At the end of the first semester the week of constant studying and taking final exams was finally over, and Ethan didn't have to be back at school until the following Wednesday.

It felt good to have some free time before he was to start his summer classes. He would often write his parents telling them that living in a dorm is nice, but there is just no privacy. Students come and go at all hours of the day and night. Phones are constantly ringing; door slamming and car horns honking fill every minute. He works part time at the local pizza shop, which enables him to save some money. He now yearns to get away from the studying, the parties, and the constant buzz of campus life.

One of his best friends on campus is Chase Watkins, who is a tall muscular guy, with blonde hair and a good sense of humor. From the first day they met, they got along very well. Chase is in his first year of med school, with hopes of becoming a doctor. Now the two friends have time on their hands and Chase has suggested that the two of them take a camping trip up into the mountains for few days, to get away from the campus.

"The wilderness in this part of the country," he tells Ethan, "is unbelievable; it is so vast, and unexplored."

Chase, who has grown up around here tells Ethan the rich history of his state. From the early days of fur trading to gold prospecting and to today's lumber industry.

Ethan tells his friend, "I haven't gone exploring in the woods since I was fourteen years old."

"Well, I guess it's time I showed you the wilderness around here," suggests Chase with excitement in his voice. Quickly agreeing on this camping trip, Ethan is hoping that it will bring back fond memories of when he was in the Boy Scouts.

Chase tells him, "Not far from here, just over the border in the State of Washington, there is a large Native American population, and they live on the Yakama Indian Reservation."

This has Ethan's attention and raising up his head quickly, he replies, "This will be awesome, I can't wait to meet them."

In a somewhat guarded way, Chase says, "I've never had an interest in going on a reservation and talking with the Native Americans, but I know that you would enjoy it."

Ethan pats his friend on the back saying, "I owe you for this one, buddy."

Yes, Ethan had always had an interest in Native American culture and traditions, with the many different tribes living in his home state of Wisconsin; however, he never really had the opportunity to get to know any of them.

Chase mentions, "Maybe we will visit a reservation on our way to the mountains."

Ethan jumps at the opportunity, now on his feet and clapping his hands. He is so excited upon hearing this that he runs out into the hallway from his room, to call his parents and tell them what he is going to do. Out in the hallway he abruptly stops and calmly comes back into the room. With a grin on his face, he tells Chase, "Maybe I should wait until after I actually go to the Indian Reservation, before calling my parents. That way," he laughs, "I will actually have something to tell my parents about my visit there."

Chase, now smiling, answers, "That would be a good idea, now let's start packing the things we are going to need."

Both young men fill their backpacks quickly, with Chase having so much stuff in his that he has trouble getting the top flap to close. After they leave their room and go outside, they next begin to load up their car with the other supplies they think they will need. While they are preoccupied with this task, they are unaware that a group of students has gathered a short distance away. Ethan looks up several times in their direction, but pays little attention to them. As it is common for students to gather outside an apartment building, especially if later there is going to be a party held there. Focusing on the task at hand, a few minutes pass when Ethan sees a girl running towards him. As she gets closer, he can see a frightened look on her face. Being the kindhearted person that he is, he stops what he is doing and asks, "What is wrong?"

She replies while holding one hand over her mouth, and as she points back towards the group of students, saying, "They are going to hurt that guy."

Upon hearing this, Ethan immediately throws down the stuff he has in his hands and without bothering to talk to Chase, he begins a quick jog in the direction that the girl pointed. When he gets there, it is apparent to him that a fight is in progress. However, as he pushes his way through the crowd, it obviously isn't a fair fight. He can see that three students are on top of one student on the ground. Ethan, being an honest and decent guy that he is, can't stand there and do nothing, so he decides to intervene. He quickly walks over and grabs one student by his shoulders, and forcibly throws him off. Swiftly reaching down again, he pulls another student off by his ankle, dragging him a short distance away. By this time, the third student has gotten up and walks over to Ethan with rage on his face. Pointing a finger he declares, "You should have minded your own business."

The enraged student, angry that someone dare interfere, now cocks his arm back ready to deliver a punch. Ethan is too quick, and he swings and delivers a punch of his own. With a crunching sound, his fist connects perfectly to the students jaw. Reeling backwards, the enraged student falls to the ground, dazed at what just happened.

Looking over, Ethan can see the student that has been the target of these three, is now starting to stand up. One of the other bullies now begins making his way back towards that student, and that is when Ethan very calmly reaches out and puts the bully in a headlock. Clamping down hard, he asks him, "You don't want to fight any more, do you?"

The student begins thrashing back and forth trying to break Ethan's grip, but to no avail. The other two bullies, back on their feet, are walking in a menacing manner towards Ethan telling him, "You are going to be sorry for interfering."

However, in a flash, the other student who had been the target of their bullying is now off the ground, and jumps on both of the bullies. Still holding the one student in a headlock, Ethan can see that this student has no problem in taking care of the two bullies all by himself. After being thoroughly humiliated, the two bullies have had enough and when they get to their feet, they both run away. Ethan releases his grip on the third one, and asks him, "Do you want to continue this fight on your own?"

Without saying a word, the student reaches down, picks up his jacket and wastes no time in running away.

By this time, a large crowd had gathered, and they are all cheering. One saying, "It is good to see those bullies finally getting what they deserve." Others tell Ethan, "Watch your back, those three bullies are constantly causing trouble."

Looking over Ethan can see this other student brushing the dirt from his pants and trying to straighten his hair.

Looking up, and with only minor cuts on his face, he says, "I'm grateful that someone had the guts to step in and help me."

Ethan walks over and introduces himself, "My name is Ethan, and it was no problem."

"My name is Joseph Browndeer."

Puzzled by the incident, Ethan asks, "Joseph, why did those students jump you?"

"Because," he replies in a harsh tone as he looks around, "I am a Native American."

Still in a guarded frame of mind, Joseph, who is now walking around and looking closely at Ethan, asks, "Do you have anything against Native Americans?"

With a bewildered expression, Ethan replies, "No, not as long as you don't have anything against someone being from Wisconsin."

Stopping, Joseph smiles, now realizing that Ethan is different from the other students he has encountered since arriving here on campus. Joseph always felt like an outcast from the very first day that he arrived here. After being shunned, ignored, and left out by all the other students, with never being invited to parties, and reading groups or even to play in any of the sport activities that took place around the dorms. Joseph is from the Yakama Indian Reservation, where he has spent his whole life. Now that he is grown up, he wants to see what is beyond the reservation. He resisted learning the ways of his people, believing that the tribal ceremonies that they do is a lot of nonsense and a waste of time. The stories and tall tales told by his grandfather only made him more determined to seek a different way of life.

His grandfather's tales of spirits, prophecies and of mystical creatures did not interest him. Joseph was different; he wanted what the white man had. He wanted to live in a big city, see the lights and to have lots of money. Yet, since arriving on campus, Joseph has encountered a type of people, which he did not have previous experience dealing with. He was the only Native American on this whole campus, and in a short time, he felt very isolated and cut off.

However, standing in front of him was someone who didn't look at him differently, and who without being asked, jumped into this fight. Joseph immediately got the feeling that Ethan was a good man, one that he could trust and depend on.

Joseph answers back with a smile on his face, "Someone from Wisconsin is ok in my book."

The two new friends laugh.

The two friends now gathered up Joseph's books, which are scattered about on the ground. As they began walking back to Ethan's car, they can see Chase standing there with his arms crossed and he says, "I would have helped, but it looked like you two had everything under control."

"I want you to meet Joseph Browndeer; he's going to hang around with us."

Ethan now introduces Chase to Joseph, "Glad to meet you," says Chase as the two shake hands.

Joseph nods his head, still cautious and a little wary about his newfound friends.

The three go back down the street and sit on the ground outside the apartment building, and talk.

With his chin up, Joseph tells them, "I'm from the Yakama Indian Tribe; it's a reservation just over the Washington state line."

His face lights up, "What a coincidence" says Ethan, "We were just talking about that Reservation."

This was a chance encounter that Ethan is most anxious to pursue. The two tell Joseph about their planned camping trip up into the mountains, and Ethan tells him in a joking manner, "I want to see a Bigfoot."

Chase laughs, but Joseph does not, he finds the remark rude. With a serious look on his face, Joseph tells them, "To my tribe this creature is more than just a myth or fable; it is a very real part of their culture."

Caught off guard by this, Ethan tries to explain, "Where I'm from, these tales of Bigfoot are amusing and humorous."

After a moment of silence, Ethan goes on to tell Joseph and Chase, "I don't believe in Bigfoot or Sasquatch, as these mystical beasts are sometimes called."

Joseph however insists, "There is some truth behind the myths and legends of these creatures, even though I myself really don't believe that the creature exists. There are many in my tribe that claims to have seen one."

At this point Joseph wants to impress his new friends, as he has found it difficult to make friends off the Reservation.

Sensing an opportunity, Joseph goes on to say, "I have listened to the stories and tales told by my relatives since I was a boy. When all of my relatives along with the rest of the tribe would come together and gather around the campfire, here they would talk of the old days. Some of my Uncles could recall the time when there was an abundance of wildlife in the area, before the white man came. Others talked of the sacred dances and rituals that they did."

Ethan is all ears, and now sits down and listens intensely, not taking his eyes off his new friend.

"Some of these dances," Joseph continues, "Are to commemorate the coming of spring, while others celebrate a good hunt. However," Joseph goes on to say with excitement in his voice, "that the most interesting stories are the ones told by the Tribal Elders. These wise old men," he says as he looks at his two new friends, "would recall that a bear hunt back in their younger days, consisted of carrying nothing more than a bow and arrows. A man, they said had to be very brave and fearless to hunt this way. With many of these hunters ending up being killed by the very animal, they were trying to kill themselves."

Impressed and in awe, Ethan tells Joseph, "This is all very fascinating to me, and someday I would like to travel to your Reservation and meet your family."

Joseph replies, "I will be proud to show my people, that there are some white men, that still have honor, and that speak with an honest tongue."

Ethan turns and now begins talking to Chase about the possibility of them visiting Josephs Reservation.

Quickly getting their attention again, "I have not told you the best stories yet," insists Joseph speaking in a loud voice.

At this time, he knew that Ethan was hanging on his every word when he would talk about mysterious creatures and other legends.

"My Ancestors," Joseph began to say, "spoke of the creatures you call Bigfoot, in my language they are called Sc'wen'ey'ti, or Shadow Beasts. Some of the tribes farther north call these creatures, "The Guardians of The Forest."

One very old Tribal Leader who must have been almost a hundred years old when I heard him recall his own encounters with the beasts."

Chase now sits down next to Ethan, beginning to show some interest in this story.

"This old Tribal Leader," Joseph continues, "says these creatures are like a supernatural being, quick and stealthy. The sight of one will freeze a man in his tracks, as if it had cast a spell over him. Many men, who claimed to have seen one, would later die an early death. As told in the legends and folklore, that the creature would take men's souls from their bodies. The body cannot survive long without its soul to guide it. The dead man's spirit will then roam the area constantly looking for its lost soul."

Hearing this, Ethan has to smile; he thought what a great story this is. Looking over at Chase it is obvious by his body language that he is a little spooked by all this talk of spirits and strange creatures.

Joseph begins to laugh, telling his friends, "These are just stories, tall tales. Nothing more than old peoples imaginations."

Ethan remains sitting, with his head lowered, still thinking about these stories.

Having amused his friends, Joseph mentions, "I'm leaving today to go and visit my relatives on the Reservation."

Looking down at Ethan and Chase and hoping he isn't being too trusting, he asks, "Would the two of you like to come with me."

Before they can answer, he goes on to say, "It isn't that far from here."

After hearing this, Ethan's face lights up even more, and he looks over at Chase and asks, "Why don't we go and camp near Josephs reservation, I think it will be awesome."

Chase does not like this as he has already had a place all picked out, one that he and Ethan were going to camp at. However, when he sees the look on Ethan's face, and how excited he is at the chance to visit a reservation, he knows that it will be a waste of time trying to talk him out of going with Joseph.

With a sneer, Chase replies, "That sounds like a great idea, let's get packing."

After discussing their trip in more detail, the three have decided to take just one vehicle. While they wait for Joseph to return with his gear, Chase and Ethan finish packing their gear into the car.

They don't have to wait long, as Joseph is fleet on his feet. With only a small backpack, he moves very quickly to join his new friends. They finish loading up the car and after getting gas, the three take turns driving. After several hours and many stories later, the three young men arrive at the Yakama Indian Reservation. A sign on the main road leading in tells them that it has a population of 8,400. They can see that many of the buildings here are old and run down, and several of them look to be abandoned.

Joseph has told his friends that unemployment on the reservation is high, and that most of the people that live here grow their own food. Now traveling farther into this old city, they can see countless teepees and totem poles. A great many of these Native Americans are riding on horseback, and they actually outnumbered the cars. Soon they stop and get out of the car, and instantly Ethan begins taking pictures and asking questions right away, he is like a kid at a museum. After introducing his two new friends to members of his reservation, Joseph tells them, "There is someone special I would like you to meet."

He takes his two friends farther onto the reservation and straight to the cabin of the oldest member of his tribe.

CHAPTER 2

As the three are walking up to the cabin, they can see an older man sitting on the front porch. Ethan notices that this is not someone dressed up to look like a Native American, as he had seen in the big cities. This is indeed a true Native American; and Ethan can tell that he is a very proud and dignified man. With his chin up and his chest out, he wears a buckskin coat with a single feather in his long black hair. With moccasins on his feet, and smoking a long pipe, he looks very natural and relaxed. When the old man sees the three young men, he quickly stands up and motions with his hand for them to come closer.

As they near the porch, Joseph then speaks up, "This man is my Grandfather, and his name is Istaqa, which means Kicking Bear in my native language."

Stepping away from his chair, "I have not seen you in some time," calls out Kicking Bear.

Nodding his head in agreement, "Hello Grandfather," replies Joseph, "I would like you to meet my friends."

Ethan eagerly steps forward to shake his hand and he stares at him for a moment before sitting down. With his eyes focused on Ethan, Kicking Bear speaks in a quiet voice, saying, "We don't get very many non-natives here. But, if you are a friend of Josephs then you are welcome here."

With that said, he reaches out and gives Ethan a hard pat on the shoulder.

A little intimidated by the strength of this old man, Ethan cracks a smile.

Joseph now begins to tell his Grandfather how Ethan had helped him in a fight he had on campus.

The old man listens patiently, and when Joseph is done he then looks back at Ethan, and tells him, "Lean closer so that I can look into your eyes."

Trying not to show how nervous he really is, Ethan does as he is told and moves closer to the old man. Not knowing for sure what to expect next. Kicking Bear, now just about a foot away stares at Ethan for a moment, a tense look is in his eyes. Then he backs up and says, "You are a good man, your heart is pure and honest."

Ethan, now a little caught off guard by these remarks, "Thank you for the kind words," and after a short pause, asks, "May we sit and talk with you for a while."

Sitting back in his chair, Kicking Bear smiles and replies, "It will make me happy if you do so."

Kicking Bear is a man that spoke very little, but in his few words, he said everything that needed to be said. Ethan, almost mesmerized, hung on every word and phrase that this Tribal Elder said.

Kicking Bear looking over at his Grandson refers to him as Shikoba. Now with a broad smile across his face says, "In the language of my people Shikoba means Little Feather."

With a devious grin, Ethan and Chase look at their friend and chuckle a little.

This nickname is one that Joseph does not like, and he strongly asks his two friends, "Do not tell anyone what you have just heard!"

The two node their heads, saying, "Not to worry, your secret is safe with us."

Chase now steps forward and introduces himself, "Hello sir, my name is Chase Watkins, it is very nice meeting you."

However, he keeps his distance, he seems a little nervous about being here. With his hands back in his pockets, and looking down, he kicks the dirt lightly.

Kicking Bear watches Chase for a moment, sensing the young man's apprehension. "You have nothing to be worried about."

Running his fingers through his hair, "Oh I'm not worried, not at all," replies Chase, as puts his hands in his pockets only to bring them right back out again.

Kicking Bear nods his head, "Your eyes give your true feelings away."

Chase doesn't know how to respond to this, and he keeps silent.

Kicking Bear talks to them for quite a long time and they learn that he is the Grandson of the famous Chief Kamaiakan, the leader of the Yakama Nation back in the mid eighteen hundreds. With a higher pitch in his voice, Kicking Bear now tells them, "You have come at a good time, a Powwow," he states, "is about to start, there will be dancing and music." He encourages them to stay and watch. He is sure they will enjoy themselves.

Ethan can't believe his luck, and he thinks it is a great opportunity to witness a real live Native American Ceremony. Chase on the other hand, is more skeptical and really doesn't want to be here.

Noticing his friends edginess, Ethan tells him, "This is going to be awesome; we'll sit and watch, nothing more."

Chase is still hesitant and uncertain, but with a lot of encouragement from Ethan, he reluctantly agrees.

Ethan looks quickly back at kicking Bear, and practically yelling says, "Yes, we will stay!"

Smiling as only an elder can, Kicking Bear now gets up and leads the three young men down a path and into the woods. After traveling a short distance, it soon opens up into something that resembles an arena. Seats are just logs on the ground placed in a great circle, and in the center is a large pile of wood stacked very high. Kicking Bear now leads them around to the opposite side; here he has them sit on the logs. Telling them, "You will stay here."

Quickly sitting down, Ethan reaches up, and grabs Chase by the arm saying, "This is going to be awesome, can you believe this?"

Looking all around, Chase bites his lip, and with a nervous tone in his voice says, "I hope you know what you're doing."

Waving his hand, "Just relax and enjoy the show, everything is going to be alright."

Kicking Bear now goes over and stands in front of a totem pole, and he seems to be chanting as he holds his arms out. Ethan and Chase watch with anxious anticipation as other members of the tribe soon begin to make their way into this arena. The noise level is starting to increase and Ethan can feel an excitement in the air. He stares as if he were a boy at a circus, it all seems so fascinating to him.

Chase glances at his watch several times, causing Ethan to tell him, "Just calm down, what are you so tense about, this is going to be fun."

Sitting very still trying not to attract any attention his way, "It's all the stories I have heard about Native Americans," answers Chase in a low whisper, "How they don't like the white man."

Ethan quickly answers, "That's nonsense, we have nothing to worry about, they seem very friendly to me. Besides, we're with Joseph, and he's our friend, he won't let anything happen to us."

Chase smiles a little, and lets out a big sigh, "Maybe your right."

"Of course I'm right," answers Ethan, as he reaches over and puts Chase in a headlock. The two fall back and wrestle on the ground for a moment, and this seems to have relaxed Chase somewhat. It is now beginning to get dark, with the last rays of the sun touching the tops of the trees, long shadows begin to cross the ground. The two young men get quiet and serious as the drums begin beating; the air now is very still. Coming from somewhere in the woods the sound of a flute can be heard along with the jingling of bells. Ethan and Chase watch keenly as warriors dressed in elaborate costumes begin making their way out of the woods. These warriors march in a single file; they are silent and look straight ahead. Lead by a gray haired elder who is wearing a full-feathered headdress, and carrying a decorated staff. Several of the warriors are carrying lit torches, and the light flickers off the nearby woods giving the scene a captivating and mystic appearance.

These warriors march right in front of Ethan and Chase, and then they form a circle around the large pile of wood. As the drums are now beginning to beat faster, these warriors start singing and dancing, and throwing their arms into the air. After several minutes, and like a well-rehearsed play, everything comes to a standstill. The drums are silent, and the singing has stopped, an eerie hush comes over this whole magnificent ceremony. Suddenly, from deep in the woods, the piercing cry of an eagle can be heard. This causes all the dancers to get down on one knee and bow their heads. A single drum now begins a slow rhythm; its solitary beat is a prelude to what is going to happen next. One of the tribe's Elders stands up, and raising his feathered staff towards the sky, he begins to chant.

After several minutes of this, he then points his staff at the large pile of wood. At that instant, everyone then sees a flaming arrow shoot down from a nearby treetop. The arrow hits the pile of wood, which soon begins to burn. In no time, the flames are reaching twenty feet into the air. This is when the drums start beating faster again and the dancers rise up and begin a slow dance circling around the fire. The women now join in and it is such an awesome sight, that Ethan is at the edge of his seat taking it all in. Chase, on the other hand, isn't so sure about all this, and by the look on his face, it is apparent that he is very uncomfortable being here. Joseph has now joined his two friends, and he asks, "Would either of you like to meet the Elders from the other tribes?"

Without hesitation, Ethan is on his feet and tells Joseph as he grabs his arm, "That will be awesome, lead the way." After taking a couple of steps and looking back he can see that Chase has remained seated.

Looking up, as his feet nervously taps the ground, "I'm okay right here, you go ahead."

Ethan, a little disappointed, but not wasting any time trying to get Chase to come along, now follows close behind Joseph. The two make their way around the dancers, who grab at Ethan in an attempt to get him to join them. All Ethan can do is smile and shrug his shoulders. Joseph takes him over and sits him on a log in front of the Elders.

Feeling intimidated yet excited, Ethan tries not to act like an adolescent. Each of these Elder Statesmen proudly introduces himself to Ethan, and they all have such colorful names. One calling himself "Wolfs Paw," another is "Eye Of Eagle."

Ethan by this time is feeling very comfortable, and the Elders seem to like him. "You have a good heart," one says while another comments, "You hold yourself up with courage and honor."

A little shocked by these comments, all Ethan can do is to thank them for their kind words.

One Elder, who has stepped closer and touching Ethan on the shoulder with his staff, speaks, "You are troubled by a strange dream, are you not?"

Taken aback by this, Ethan needs to take a deep breath, he had nearly forgotten about the dreams he had last summer. It bothered him that this Elder knew this, as he has never told anyone. Before he can question the Elder, Joseph's Grandfather, Kicking Bear, who is also sitting there, hands Ethan a cup and says, "This is spirit water, it will open your soul, and that you will be able to see many things that others cannot."

Still spooked, Ethan figures that this is just some homemade brew, he is hoping that it will calm his nerves. Therefore, he begins drinking the spirit water and listing to more of their stories. He hears so many interesting and fascinating stories, he wishes that he had brought along his tape recorder. After awhile he begins to get light headed, this he tells himself, must be some strong alcohol, even if Josephs Grandfather says it is spirit water. The words coming from the elders now seem to be gibberish, and Ethan shakes his head several times. A cool sensation covers his body, and he begins breathing in very short and shallow breaths. After several more minutes, things around him start to get fuzzy. He begins to squint his eyes in an attempt to see better, when suddenly he feels someone grab his arm. He's now swiftly picked up from the log he is sitting on, and pulled out among the dancers circling the fire. His head is by now spinning, with the noise and everyone moving around him so fast it all seems surreal. Trying his best to imitate his hosts, he moves with them as they circle the fire.

While lost in this frenzy of activity, he now begins to notice not far from him, there is a man with the head of a bear, another man has the head of a mountain lion. He again squints his eyes to see better, but the heads look very real to him, not like a mask. The people with the animal heads now start to circle around him, and one would rush in and then would just as quickly back away. As Ethan is circling around the fire, his arms swing loosely at his sides. Doing his best to keep up with those around him, he feels carefree, and completely immersed in this ceremony. In a state of being totally relaxed, it is serene and peaceful, as he has never felt before.

As the noise begins to get faint, he is startled when he now feels himself beginning to float up in the air. After a moment, he is looking down at everyone, but no one seems to pay any attention to him.

It all seems so outlandish, like a dream or more like an out of body experience. Straining to gain control of his senses, he tries telling himself, "This can't really be happening."

Ethan tries shaking his head, but this only causes things to become even more confusing and mystifying.

As he leans back and takes a quick glance up at the night sky, he notices that the stars seem to be extremely bright tonight. He then notices several of these stars begin to move across the sky, and then they move back the other way. Ethan is now completely mesmerized by this, and unable to comprehend what is going on. Soon he sees all the stars in the sky moving, as if they are waves on a pond. Hundreds of stars flow effortlessly from right to left and then back again. How very strange this is to him, and young Ethan has no clue as to why the stars would move as they are. When he leans forward again, and looks around, he is astounded to find himself, once again sitting back in front of the Elders. With eyes wide open, he is now confused and bewildered at what has just happened. He has been drunk many times before this, but he has never hallucinated.

Remaining perfectly still, as he is trying to shake off the effects of the spirit water. He swallows hard, and tenses up as a medicine man now approaches him. Standing directly in front of Ethan he asks, "Do you want to cross over into the spirit world," but he adds waving his hands, "It will only be for a brief time."

Ethan is by now feeling very good at this point, and with his inhabitations lowered he smiles and tells the Medicine Man, "Sure, let's do this."

Knowing full well, you only go into this so-called Spirit World after you have died. However, as he begins to think about this, it causes him to have second thoughts about agreeing to it.

As he is being escorted away by a brave on each side of him, he knows it is too late to back out now. After walking a short distance, this Medicine Man stops and hands Ethan a cup and Ethan drinks its contents without questioning it. Wiping his mouth with his sleeve, he hands the cup back. The contents of this drink is something he has never tasted before, it is bitter sweet. After coughing several times, he stands straight, his legs feeling slightly unsteady.

The Medicine Man tells Ethan, "What you have just drank, will enable your spirit to leave your body."

Ethan feels no fear or panic, as his overpowering curiosity takes over, and he nods his head in agreement. He is guided over to a totem pole that is not far away, and here he is told to put both his hands on it. After doing this, he watches as the Medicine Man backs up and begins to chant as he is shaking a rattle. Ethan feels a little silly at this point, and he figures they are playing a joke on him, and at any moment, everyone will start laughing. As he stands there with a grin on his face, in the semi darkness, his head still fuzzy and unclear, he awaits what is next. He is surprised as he watches a white fog slowly come out of the dark woods and it soon surrounds him. It is so thick that he can see no one, and he no longer can hear the beating of the drums. All is silent; it gives him an eerily feeling of impending doom. The grin quickly leaves his face, "If this is a joke," he asks himself, "how did they make that fog appear?"

Suddenly the fog parts to his right, and he is startled when he can see a great grassy plain open up before his eyes. It stretches for as far as he can see, and not far away there is a heard of buffalo, and they are kicking up great amounts of dust. He can also see Indians on horseback riding alongside these buffalo. There must be a dozen of them, and they are shooting their bow and arrows at the buffalo. Suddenly the fog closes, and the scene is gone as quickly as it had appeared. Ethan begins to breathe much faster now, but the fog parts again, this time right In front of him. He can now see several teepees in the distance, and with smoke rising up from a few campfires, it reminds him of a picture he once saw. Then just like the first image, the fog closes in on this scene, only to open up to his left. Looking in that direction he can see a field of tall grass leading out to the edge of a forest. However, there is something in the distance, it is a large animal, and it is standing on two legs.

To Ethan it looks like a gorilla, only this creature is much bigger, and its eyes seemed fixed directly on him. Ethan is speechless as to what to do next, as he tries to understand the meaning of the things that he has just witnessed. He watches with panic as this large animal now begins to walk towards him, and it is walking just like a man walks. Suddenly Ethan's mouth drops and the hair on the back of his neck now stands up and he breaks out into a cold sweat. What he is looking at is the same as the vision that he saw in his dreams, and also on the book cover. This has shocked Ethan, he wants to move away, but can't, it is as if his body is frozen. He is even unable to call out, this makes him feel very helpless, and his body feels as if is paralyzed. As this creature gets closer, Ethan begins to get more upset, he has seen enough of this Spirit World. At that moment, he feels someone grab his arm and pull him backwards. As soon as he lets go of the totem pole everything suddenly changes back to the way it was. The white fog is now gone, and he can now hear the drums beating once again. He takes two steps back and then falls to the ground. Dazed for a second, he suddenly feels two sets of hands grab him. As the warriors pick up Ethan, he finds himself too exhausted to walk. They must carry him back over near the fire. Here he is sat down on a log in front of the Tribal Elders.

All of these Elders are looking at him, but Ethan can only stare back. Feeling like he's in a dream, he struggles to understand all of this.

After a moment of silence, one of the Elders asks, "What have you seen in the Spirit World?"

Ethan sits there starring straight ahead with his mouth open, unable to speak. Blinking his eyes several times, he realizes that he is breathing very fast and his legs are shaking.

Looking up with a blank stare, "What just happened to me," he asks in a quivering voice, "did I just have an out of body experience?" He now shakes his head several times, trying to make sense of the apparitions that he saw.

Now slowly, he begins to tell the Tribal Elders about the fog, and how when it parted, he could see the buffalo and the teepees.

They all sit there with a mute look on their faces; as if they know he has more to tell them. After another moment, Ethan mentions to the Elders, "I saw a hairy creature that stood on two legs."

Upon hearing this, the Elders seem startled and begin talking among themselves. Kicking Bear turns towards Ethan and says, "Rarely does anyone see a Sc'wen'ey'ti, especially a white man"

With a pinched forehead, Ethan doesn't know what he is talking about. Kicking Bear seeing the confused look on Ethan's face, replies that, "A Sc'wen'ey'ti is the one we call the Guardian of The Forest, the one the white man calls Big Foot."

With an innocent expression, he looks up into the faces of these Tribal Elders; Ethan politely asks them, "What does it means to see this guardian figure?"

Now sitting closer, Kicking Bear answers, "It means you will see him again in the future, sometimes it is a bad omen, sometimes it's not, you will have to wait and find out."

With a stern look, Wolf's Paw speaks up, "You have been blessed with the sight of the sacred beast. When the time comes, do not turn your back on it."

Now Ethan is thinking that they put a curse on him, and this he wants no part of.

Kicking Bear moves even closer to him and putting his hand on his shoulder says, "Do not be afraid, our ancestral warriors will protect you."

He's not sure how to interpret this, still hoping that it was all a dream or hallucination.

After his head clears, Ethan now stands up and walks back over to where Chase is sitting, and still very confused at what has just happened to him. He looks at Chase and asks, "Did you see everything that happened to me over there?"

Chase looks at him with an odd expression on his face and replies, "What do you mean?"

Ethan blinks his eyes several times and replies, "Didn't you see the people with the animal heads, and then I was floating."

Sitting back, Chase laughs, and tells him, "You must be drunk."

Waving his hand, "No," Ethan quickly answers, "I'm not drunk, it was all real, what about the stars, didn't you see them move?"

With a sneer, "No" answers Chase, "they look just like ordinary stars to me."

Now Ethan is getting nervous, putting his hand on his chin, trying to come up with an explanation, he asks himself, "Could this have all been a hallucination?"

Looking back at Chase, "What about when I was standing in front of that totem pole," demands Ethan, now a little angry, "and the white fog that came in from the woods, you had to have seen that?"

Shaking his head, "No," answers Chase, "I didn't see anything, all I saw is that you went over and started talking to the Tribal Leaders, that lasted a few minutes and then you came straight back over here."

Needing a minute to calm down, by now, Ethan is thinking that it was something in the drink, some kind of mind-altering drug that caused him to hallucinate and become delusional. It takes him quite a while to feel comfortable again, as the recent events race through his mind. The rest of the ceremony continues, and it lasts late into the night.

Up early the next morning, Ethan is still curious about the previous night's strange activities. He walks over to Kicking Bears cabin, hoping to learn in more detail exactly about what occurred.

Kicking Bear is sitting on his front porch, smoking his pipe and he watches as young Ethan approaches. Sensing that the young man is very troubled and concerned by what he saw and had experienced the previous night. Motioning for Ethan to sit down, the two sit in silence for several minutes.

Ethan is hesitant to ask what is on his mind; maybe Kicking Bear will think he is mocking their sacred ceremonies. With his forehead pinched, and his hands constantly moving, Ethan is about to say something.

However, Kicking Bear speaks first, "I see in your eyes that you are troubled and upset, you have questions that need answers."

Nodding his head in agreement as he hasn't found the right words or the right questions to ask.

Kicking Bear studies the young man closely, watching his every move. "I will tell you what you have come seeking," he says in a low voice.

Ethan isn't sure at this time if he even wants to know the answers, maybe it should be left alone.

Leaning forward in his chair, Kicking Bear tells him, "The hairy creature that you saw last night, the one that my people call a Sc'wen'ey'ti, or Shadow Beast. That these Shadow Beasts will only show themselves if they choose to be seen, otherwise they move about unnoticed as if somehow they can make themselves invisible."

Ethan knows that Kicking Bears words have come from his heart, and that he is an honest and truthful man. He also knows that what Kicking Bear is telling him, is what he truly believes, and that this folk lore about mystical beasts is a part of the culture of the Indians that live in this part of the country.

Realizing that this is the right time to open up about his dreams, Ethan replies, "Before coming here, I had several dreams about a hairy creature, and it looked exactly like the creature I saw last night. Can you tell me what it all means?"

Kicking Bear now sitting back in his chair begins to rub his chin. Looking at Ethan he says, "There is something special about you, for the Shadow Beast to visit you in your dreams is very rare."

Ethan, hearing this now begins running his fingers through his hair, he swallows hard and asks, "So what is so special about me that this Shadow Beast would single me out, why not someone from this Reservation?"

Kicking Bear leans forward again, and putting his hand on Ethan's shoulder looks him straight in the eyes and replies, "You have been chosen by the Great Spirit, for what purpose, only he knows."

Ethan, now a little uneasy has to ask Kicking Bear, "Have you ever seen one of these so-called Shadow Beast yourself?"

Sitting back in his chair, and with a quick smile, holding up two fingers, Kicking Bear replies, "Twice in my life I have seen this creature."

Feeling that he must learn more, Ethan now makes himself more comfortable and he watches as this old wise man sits back up in his chair. His eyes staring straight out into nowhere, and he begins by saying, "The young people in my tribe do not believe in the stories of the Shadow Beasts, they have chosen the ways of the white man. That," he says after a short pause, "is why they cannot see the Shadow Beast." Looking at Ethan, he says, "I mean no disrespect, only that our two cultures are very different."

He nods slowly, and after a moment of silence, Ethan again asks Kicking Bear, "Would you please recall for me, your two encounters with these, Guardians of The Forest?"

Ethan is by now on the edge of his seat and his feet are constantly tapping the floor. Never has a story captivated him so thoroughly, and he feels very strange as he listens to the words.

With a soft-spoken voice, Kicking Bear begins to tell Ethan of the first time he saw a Shadow Beast. "It was when I was just a boy," he begins "that I was maybe ten years old at the time. While fishing with my father on the Wenatchee River, a foul smell filled the air. I at first thought it was from a dead animal, but as I looked around, I noticed something on the nearby riverbank. It was maybe only a hundred yards away, I could see a very big man standing on the shore. However, as I looked closer I could see that this man was wearing a fur coat and a fur hat. How odd it seemed to me, because the weather at the time was warm, there was no need to dress like that."

Kicking Bear now gets up and moves to a different chair, the look on Ethan's face, with his hands constantly moving tells Kicking Bear that this young man truly likes listening to his stories, and a smile crosses his old weathered face. Kicking Bear continues saying, "I shouted over to my father to look in the direction that I was pointing. My father upon seeing this figure began chanting an old Indian prayer, and the two of us watched as this Shadow Beast turned and walked gently into the forest. It stopped once, turning its head and looking at us, and then it disappeared into the thick tangle of trees. My father then explained to me what I had just seen, saying, "It is a special gift when one of these Shadow Beasts chooses to make itself visible in your presence."

"My second encounter," continues Kicking Bear, as he stares out into the distance, "came many years later, while I was hunting high in the mountains with other members of the tribe. We had set up our camp not far from the base of a great mountain. We had been hunting for many days, bringing back to the camp much meat and many hides. However, on one particular day, and against the advice of the others, who said that the weather was too bad to hunt and that we should wait until tomorrow when it clears. I however, being young and anxious to prove that I was a brave hunter, chose to go anyways. I went up into the mountains alone in search of elk. My inexperience and youth got the better of me, and soon I found myself caught in a blizzard. While I was foolishly trying to move around in weather that was so bad that I couldn't see but only a few feet in front of me. I had missed placed my steps while walking across a ridge, and I slipped and tumbled down into a gorge. Here I suffered a broken leg. I knew I was in serious trouble, and I tried making my way out of the gorge and back to the camp. After several hours, I was exhausted and limping badly on my broken leg. With the temperature around zero, and the snow being so deep that even without this injury it would have been very difficult to get very far. I had made a second mistake by not bringing adequate supplies with me. It was at this moment I knew I wasn't going to make it back to the camp.

Therefore, I began a chant that my Grandfather had taught me. In this chant, I asked the Spirits of our Ancestors to come and lead me to the sacred hunting grounds of the Great Spirit. While I was preparing myself for death, I lay down and closed my eyes. The cold was closing in on me, and I knew that my time here on Mother Earth was soon ending. As I began to slip into unconsciousness, I could feel myself being picked up and carried. Thinking at first that the Great Spirit has come for me, and now I was being taken to the heavens. I felt very peaceful, and soon I could feel myself being laid down onto the ground. Opening my eyes, it was apparent that I wasn't where I thought I should be. I was now lying on the ground in front of one of the tents at the camp. As I turned my head to the side, I could see a large dark figure walking away from me, it stopped briefly and looked back at me, and then it turned and disappeared into the blizzard. I called for my friends to come out, and upon seeing me they all said they had given up hope of ever seeing me again. Once inside, I told them about how the Shadow Beast had carried me down from the mountain, that it had saved my life."

With a grin, Kicking Bear goes on and says, "Shadow Beasts are kind hearted and will help those in need, but they also can become very angry. My Grandfather told me that legend says that if any harm comes to one of these Shadow Beasts, the others of their kind will seek revenge, and they will stop at nothing."

Now Ethan finds himself totally engrossed in this story, not once taking his eyes off Kicking Bear.

"In all my years, I have only heard of one incident in which one of these Shadow Beasts has hurt anyone."

Ethan is getting more fascinated with this story with each passing minute, and now practically begs Kicking Bear, "Please tell me about that one incident, you can't stop now."

Kicking Bear is a great storyteller and he knows when he has someone's full attention, this made him happy.

However, just then Joseph walks in and with a sneer on his face, remarks "Don't tell me you believe my Grandfathers stories, he loves to spook people with his tales of the Mysterious Shadow Beasts."

Ethan can see by the depressing look on Kicking Bears face that this talk from his grandson really disappoints him.

Speaking up, Ethan tells Joseph, "I enjoy listening to your grandfather's stories and you should show more respect to him."

Joseph just shakes his head and replies, "Go ahead and be fooled by this old story teller, I've got other things to do," and he turns and walks out the door.

Kicking Bear who is now looking down at the ground, says in sad voice, "My grandson does not believe in the Shadow Beasts, that is why he will never see one."

Ethan speaks up and tells Kicking Bear, "You have to admit that it is a story that is hard to believe, unless you actually see one for yourself."

Shaking his head and rubbing his knees, "My grandson has resisted learning the ways of our people; he wants nothing to do with his native roots."

Ethan can see how sad and depressed this makes Kicking Bear, so he speaks up saying, "Don't give up on Joseph, he will realize someday how wrong he has been to turn away from his native heritage."

Kicking Bear looks up and smiles saying, "You must have some Indian blood in you to talk with such wisdom."

With a big grin, Ethan replies, "I don't think I have any, but times like this I wish I did."

"Enough about Joseph," Ethan quickly exclaims impatiently, "now tell me about the one time that one of these Shadow Beasts hurt someone."

Kicking Bear seemed to relax now and he sits back in his chair, and rubbing his chin, he begins by saying, "Many years ago, before I was born, My Grandfather told me the time when fur traders had come into these woods and onto our Reservation. There was enough game here for everyone, and my Ancestors did not object to their intrusion. However in the weeks that followed, members of the tribe found many of their traps stolen or broken. Some canoes were even missing. One day when our men were bringing furs back to our village, they tell of encountering these Fur Traders. They say that the fur traders pointed their rifles at them and took all of their furs. After many more of these incidents, the Elders agreed, that these white men have to leave this area. Several of our Elders then went to the fur trader's camp to tell them they were no longer welcomed here and that they had to leave. In response to that, the Elders are threatened and pushed around. With the fur traders saying that if they catch any Indians near their camp, they would kill them.

Therefore, the Elders wanting to avoid any bloodshed had told all the members of their tribe to stay clear of the fur trader's camp. All was peaceful for several weeks, until one of our young ones came running into the village saying that the fur traders had taken his sister. The Elders all knew just what the fur traders had in mind, and this they all agreed upon, would not be allowed to happen. All the Braves gathered around the fire and with war paint on their faces, they set out to fight the fur traders, and to rescue the girl.

These braves moved very swiftly and quietly through the forest, not wanting to alert the fur traders of their approach. Arriving on a small ridge overlooking the fur trader's camp, the braves could see no movement in the camp below. Slowly the braves made their way down, and when they got to the center of the camp, they could see four of the fur traders lying on the ground. All of these men looked like they had been beaten very badly, with torn clothing and blood everywhere. Looking closer the braves realized that all of these men were in fact dead. The girl was quickly found, as she was hiding in one of the tents nearby; she was unharmed, but very frightened. When they asked her what had happened to the fur traders, she tells of these men first kidnapping her, then tying her hands and legs. She said that they brought her here to their camp, and while lying inside the tent, she could hear a lot of shouting outside. Thinking it is members of her tribe coming to free her, she began screaming for help. Then she heard several gunshots, and the fur traders were yelling things like "Kill it, and "It's a monster."

She said after crawling over to the opening in the tent and looking out, she saw a huge hairy creature attacking these men. This creature stood on two legs and was much taller than any man she had ever seen. Dark fur covered its body, and its arms hung down to its knees. She watched; as the fur trader's guns were useless against it. She said she saw them shoot it many times but the creature never stopped. It continued attacking these men until all but one was lying motionless on the ground, this one man managed to run into the woods and she saw the creature go after him."

Kicking Bear continued saying, "That the four dead fur traders lying on the ground had a look of freight on their faces, and the body of the fifth one had been found a short distance away. Many large footprints were found, and they sank into the ground further than our own, suggesting that the creature weighed as much as three times the weight as one of them.

Once back at the village, the Elders are told at what had been found. They all immediately agreed that a Shadow Beast had come to the rescue of the girl."

After a short pause, Kicking Bear goes on to say, "The Indian prophecies say that these Shadow Beasts come from the hollow Earth; and it is there that they keep the spirits of our dead warriors."

Ethan, mesmerized, now sits back, and looking past Kicking Bear, he seems to be thinking about this amazing story just told to him. How it sounds so real and genuine, and he wishes that it were true.

Joseph and Chase now come walking into Kicking Bears cabin telling Ethan, "It is time to go, we want to be at the place that we picked out to set up our campsite before it gets dark."

Turning and making a face, "What's the rush," asks Ethan?

"Because," answers Joseph in a stern tone, "It is going to be a five hour drive from here, and then a three hour hike into the woods to the camp site."

Also anxious to get going, "Let's get their before dark," insists Chase.

Kicking bear, now looking up at Joseph, and inquisitively asks him, "Just where is this place located that you are going too."

Joseph replies, "Near Wauconda, we are planning to camp there a few days."

Kicking Bear upon hearing his grandson say this becomes concerned, and he tells them, "You should camp closer to the Reservation, there's no need to go so far away."

Joseph doesn't understand why his grandfather wants him and his friends to camp nearby.

In a rude manner, he replies, "I'm a man now, and I can go where I choose."

Kicking Bear, hearing the arrogance in his grandsons talk, now reminds him, "There are many things in the forest that you do not know about."

Joseph looks at his Grandfather and with a half grin says, "You mean things like Spirits and Ghost Warriors, and oh yes let's not forget about the Shadow Beasts, what fairy tale would be complete without them."

This talk from his grandson has now angered Kicking Bear, and he says in a harsh voice, "Just beware young man."

CHAPTER 3

As the three walk out of the cabin, Ethan says his goodbyes to Kicking Bear and to other members of the tribe. Stopping and turning around, he tells Kicking Bear, "I would like to hear more stories when I come back this way if you don't mind."

Kicking Bear just smiles and nods his head, wishing them all a safe trip. The three now finish packing their gear into the car and begin their journey north, hoping it will be pleasant weather and they all can relax before returning to school for another hectic year.

The three of them travel north on Highway 28, and in Wenatchee they merge onto Highway 97. Now the wilderness is getting much denser, and the towns are much smaller and farther apart. They finally stop in the last town on the map, a small town called Brewster. Here they decide to get gas and something to eat. While the three are standing around stretching their legs, several people come over and tell them about strange happenings going on around the town of Wauconda. Joseph who knows that Wauconda is nothing more than a ghost town; and that everyone left there when the mines shut down, and that was at least fifty years ago. These people begin to speak with shakiness in their voices, which sometimes verged on the edge of hysteria. They tell the three young college students, "There has been a wild man seen in that area, and it is best that you stay away from there."

Smiling and not wanting to get these people anymore upset than they already are, "We'll think about it," replies Ethan, "thanks for the warning."

After these people walk away the three young men chuckle at the thought of a wild man running around in the woods.

"Maybe it's Tarzan," suggests Chase, who while laughing begins to mimic the call that Tarzan made from the old movies.

"Or it could be a drunk college student," says Joseph as he staggers around. The three laugh at such foolish talk, and soon their voices grow louder.

At this time, they stop horsing around when they notice a very peculiar man come out of the gas station. Walking a short distance, he begins stacking firewood next to an old fence. This man seems very nervous, and after a moment, he stops what he is doing and gives the three a long cold look.

The three instantly get a bad feeling about this man, there is something not right about him.

"We should be going," suggests Joseph as he motions for the others to get in the car.

However, the strange man soon approaches them, and in a very panicky voice, "You young fellers shouldn't be going up in those mountains."

Not wanting to be told where he can and can not go, Joseph replies, "What's wrong with going to the mountains, it's not like it's the dead of winter where we could get trapped by an avalanche."

The strange man now rubbing his hand over his unshaven face, constantly blinking his eyes says, "Nothin but evil up there, I should know I came face to face with the beast. After that I never step another foot in them woods again, not ever."

Now the three were intrigued, and Ethan asks, "Tell me about this beast that you saw."

Pulling out a handkerchief from his pocket and wiping the sweat from his face, the man looks around quickly, as if expecting something to happen.

Looking at the three with eyes wide open, he puckers his lips several times. It is obvious that this man has not shaved in more than a week, and with his tattered clothing the man had the appearance of a homeless person.

"You might think I'm just tryin to scare you city folks," he says as he constantly rubs his hands together. "But I know what I saw, call me a crazy man or even a lunatic, but that don't change what I saw. No sir, you three need to know about that creature that lives up there, you need to be warned. A terrible sight it is, just one look at it can cause a man to lose his nerve. The smell of the beast is terrible, just terrible, I tell folks it smells like rotting flesh. But that's my opinion, just beware, some of the Indians say the beast has magical powers. You know they worship the dam thing, it ain't nothing to be praying to, no sir it's pure evil."

The three now begin to get an uneasy feeling listening to this story; looking at each other no one says a word. The look on their faces gives away the concern and apprehension they are really feeling.

Now after a short pause the man continues, "Legend says it will take your soul, and your spirit will wonder the Earth for eternity."

Ethan and Chase are completely mystified by the mans story, however Joseph just shakes his head as he has heard these stories many times while growing up.

The man can tell he has a captive audience in the two young men, and wastes no time in continuing. Now sitting with his back against the wall, looking up he says, "About eight months ago I was scouting up on the north slope," he began with unsteady words, "just me and my dog Tanner."

After making a sharp noise, a rather skinny dog with its head lowered walks out of the shop and sits next to the man. "This be my dog Tanner," he says while patting the dog on its head. Looking up into the sky, the man seems to be confused at what he was just talking about. Shaking his head and snapping his fingers, "I was tellin you the story about the beast wasn't I," "Lets see, I was up on the North Slope, when suddenly Tanner runs ahead of me, this put me on alert, cause my dog ain't afraid of nothing. I've had him huntin bear, deer and wild boar, and one time he even tangled with a grizzly. He was takin a terrible mauling but wouldn't back down. I had to shoot and kill the bear, else he would have eaten ole Tanner. Anyways, suddenly ole Tanner came runnin and went right past me with his tail between his legs. I knew something strange must be up ahead, so I gripped my rifle real tight. As I got to the crest of the hill, I saw something about twenty yards away. Looked like a gorilla but it didn't walk on all fours like a gorilla do. No sir, this creature walked upright on two legs, I couldn't believe what I was lookin at. I stood dumbfounded, what the hell am'I lookin at, I asked myself. Then suddenly this creature turned and looked directly at me, its eyes seem to go right into me, I was instantly petrified. My hands and legs began to shake, my heart was beating so fast I thought I was havin a heart attack. I have never been so scared in my life. I turned around and started runnin, my legs were stiff, like when you get really cold and it's hard to run very fast. That's what it was like, and all I could think about is if I drop my rifle this creature will get me. I never stopped till I got back here, I found Tanner hiding inside, he wouldn't come out for nothing. "

The three can tell that just recalling his encounter with the beast has the man in near hysterics, constantly wiping the sweat from his forehead and tapping his feet on the ground. He now constantly watches the woods, his eyes twitching back and forth, and a shiver races through his body.

"Neither one of us has set foot back in them woods sense, and I don't ever plan to again the rest of my life."

At that moment a man walks by saying, "Don't pay Ed no never mind, he just up and lost his nerve one day. Yep old Ed won't go near the woods and won't go outside at night, just scared down to his bones."

Ethan is totally engrossed in the mans story, while Chase is obviously very uncomfortable as he has by this time taken several steps backwards.

"Let's go you guys," yells Joseph who is already in the car.

The man gets up and walks towards the doorway, glancing back over his shoulder he says, "You young fellers just watch your selves, cause the creature don't make no noise. It moves about like it floats on air, you might walk right by it and won't see it. If you're smart you'll turn around and head back the way you came." Now making a sharp noise the dog gets up and follows him inside.

Ethan and Chase look at one another; the uncertainty of what they were just told is on their faces. A moment later they are startled out of their trance, by the car horn blowing, the two make their way over to Joseph.

After the three get back into their car, Joseph tells his two friends, "People in this part of the state make up stories like that just to scare visitors away. They don't like strangers coming onto their land and disturbing the peace." He goes on to say, "The very place that these people claim there is a wild man; just happens to be the place that we will be sitting up our camp."

Swallowing hard, Chase asks in a rather nervous voice, "Could there really be a wild man living around here?"

With a chuckle, "Not a chance," answers Joseph, "the only thing around here is bears and deer, sorry no monsters or wild men."

The three break out laughing; Chase and Ethan now begin wrestling in the back seat and nearly causing Joseph to run off the road. After calming down, the three sit quietly starring at the scenery.

This kind of talk has them all secretly a little anxious to get there even more so than before. Glad that he had brought his camera, Ethan now jokes that he may actually get to see a Bigfoot after all.

Chase sits quietly, and by his reaction to this news, he is obviously bothered by the thought that something strange is going on around the area they are going to be camping in.

Joseph, who has lived his life listening to stories like this, tells his friends, "I'm not intimidated at all by these made up stories. Do not believe those people back at the rest stop. It is nothing more than made up stories; that I can promise you."

Hoping he is right, Chase and Ethan nonetheless stare out the window in silence. In deep thought, Ethan now recalls that Kicking Bear told him that he would at sometime in the future see this creature again. Not wanting to believe these stories, but also not wanting to cast them aside as nonsense either. Unknowing, he is grinding his teeth, a nervous habit that he does only when he is worried. This habit causes Chase to look at his friend and ask, "I didn't think you were bothered by all this talk of wild men and strange happenings?"

Pausing before looking over, his fingers tapping the armrest, Ethan has a troubled look on his face.

"I have a peculiar feeling that I can't explain," he answers as he leans his head back. "It's not a sense of danger or anything terrible, but that something extraordinary is going to happen."

Chase nods his head, "Yeah, I got a weird feeling too."

With a quick wink, Ethan says, "Everything is going to be alright."

Now trying to lighten things up, "If we have to we'll tie you up and leave you at the campsite, that should give me and Joseph time to get away," he says while trying to hold back a laugh.

Breaking out into a chuckle, "Now I feel much better," answers Chase with a sneer, and quickly he and Ethan begin wrestling again.

A little more relaxed, they now drive for several more hours, with no more talk about wild men. The roads in this part of the state are no longer paved, but just dirt trails. Just wide enough for two cars, with some stretches down to only a single lane.

Straining his neck for a better look, "This type of wilderness," Ethan says with enthusiasm, "I have never seen before."

He gazes in amazement at how tall the trees are, and the forests stretch for as far as he can see. Not a telephone pole in sight and no houses either, and they have not seen another car in a very long time. At one point, they have to stop to let a herd of elk cross the road, another time a tree has fallen across the road and the three have to push it to the side so they can continue. They finally have to stop when the road comes to a dead end.

Turning around in his seat, Joseph tells them, "From here, we will have to backpack our gear into the woods to the campsite."

"Which," he adds, "is about a fifteen-mile hike?"

Feeling exhausted from the long drive, Chase speaks up saying, "We should just camp right here, this looks like a good spot to me."

Ethan kids him saying, "If you hadn't brought so much stuff along, your back pack wouldn't be so heavy." Ethan now jokingly tells his friend, "For such a big guy, carrying that backpack should be a piece of cake for you."

Before Chase can answer, Joseph speaks up and says, "Come on, it will only take us a few hours to get there and then we can relax and enjoy the peace and quiet of nature."

Chase gives them both a stern look, and with the wave of his hand, he motions for them to lead the way. Joseph takes the lead, as he is the only one that knows the location of their camp. They walk single file down a narrow path, and it obvious that no one has used it for a very long time. The grass is at times knee high and because of the over growth of the trees it is sometimes difficult for them to fine the path. However, Joseph being a Native American is very knowledgeable in the woods, and he seems to have no problem keeping on the path. He has spent his entire life here, and the only time spent away is now that he is in college.

They stop several times to rest, and during one of these stops, they hear a strange noise from deep in the woods. It sounds like "whoop—whoop."

Standing up quickly, Joseph says with a startled look on his face, "I have never heard such a sound before; no animal I know of can make that type of noise."

"Stop trying to scare us," calls out Chase, "you know what kind of animal that was."

However, with a straight face Joseph replies, "I'm serious guys, I do not know what made that noise." He continues scanning the area, his eyes searching for any signs of the source of the noise.

The two smile as they believe their friend is joking and Ethan answers, "You can't scare us, we know you don't believe in monsters, you said so yourself."

Giving the woods a long stare, Joseph nods his head and says, "You're right, just an animal that I haven't heard in a long time."

Ethan and Chase don't think much of it, and the three now pickup up their backpacks and continue walking.

Joseph doesn't want to alarm his friends, but he is getting an awkward feeling, one he has never felt before. Disturbed by this sensation, he tries to put the thoughts out of his head.

Now continuing their trek down the path, the three are spread out by about twenty feet between each of them. Realizing that his shoe is untied, Chase curses, "Dam it, one of these days I'm going to throw away these shoes."

Ethan laughs, "You have been saying that for months."

Giving him a mean look, Chase gets down on one knee and quickly ties his shoe. While standing back up, he sees a movement in the brush just ahead. His skin gets cold, suddenly nervous, but not sure why. After all, the movement could be from any number of animals that live around here. Nevertheless, a strange feeling overcomes him, one that puts him on guard. Trying to shake off this intuition, he continues walking, maybe a little more cautious than before.

"Nothing to be afraid of," he repeats to himself. Holding his rifle a little closer to his side, and tapping his finger on the on rear sight, he realizes that the gap between him and Ethan has widened.

Chase is in the rear, and as they round a sharp curve in the trail, Ethan takes a quick look back, and he has lost sight of him, so he yells up to Joseph, "Wait a minute, I don't see Chase."

At this very instant they hear Chase yell, and looking back, they see him running around the curve towards them as if he has just seen a ghost. His arms are swinging wildly at his sides, eyes wide open and he's breathing very heavily. When he gets to them, he stops and grabs a hold of Ethan. Pointing back with a shaking finger, he shouts, "I saw something big and black standing in the woods looking at me!"

Trying to comfort him, Joseph speaks up saying, "It was just a black bear, that's all nothing more."

Shaking his head vigorously, "No" insists Chase, his voice becoming louder, "that was no bear, its face was flat, and I saw it reach up and grab a tree branch, it had fingers not claws."

Joseph replies, "You must still be spooked by the stories that those people we had met earlier had told us, they just wanted to scare us, that's all it is."

Ethan can see the fear on Chases face, and the sweat on his hands as he walks back and forth. What he saw, Ethan isn't sure, but he doesn't believe in wild men, or Bigfoot or any other large hairy creature living in these or any other woods, they just don't exist. Chase is so upset, he now wants to go back to the car; he wants no part of this camping trip any longer.

Joseph convinces him, "It will be dark before you can make it back to the car and that it is dangerous to be in these woods after dark. "You will get lost," Joseph ardently tells him, "and no one would ever find you." Joseph reminds them, "We are probably the only ones in this area," and looking around he says, "This area consists of several hundred square miles."

Ethan believes he is right, they haven't seen anyone since that small town they stopped in, and that was hours ago.

They are truly in a no man's land, if anyone were to get lost or injured in these woods, it could very well be a death sentence for them. Cell phones don't work here, and there are no rangers patrolling on horseback. If not for Joseph, they wouldn't even be able to find their way back to the car. Just too many trails like the one they are following, no way to know the right one from the wrong one.

Chase, after hearing his friend explain the dangers of being alone out here, reluctantly agrees and the three now continue as Joseph leads the way. Chase has by now; calmed down a bit, he is still looking around nervously and telling the others that he did see a hairy monster. Ethan tells him, "Let it go, whatever it was that you saw is now way behind us."

Joseph suggests, "This would be a good time to load our rifles, as there are bears in these woods."

Now with loaded rifles on their shoulders, they walk with a little more confidence. Chase is now walking very close to Ethan, still mumbling about what he saw.

After another hour of hiking, they finally reach their camping site. In a small clearing just off the path, it appears to be the perfect spot. Surrounded by tall trees, and thick bushes, the ground is flat here, idea for putting up their tents on. In the center is a small circle of rocks; the burnt pieces of wood indicate that this is where there fire will be. It is everything that Ethan was hoping it would be. He gazes at its simple beauty, rustic yet alluring. They have just enough time to set up their tents and gather firewood before it gets dark. With the last rays of sunshine leaving the sky turning it an orange color, the three settle down around the campfire. The woods have all the familiar sounds that Ethan can remember while growing up in Wisconsin. He can hear the hoot of the night owl, the frogs with their constant chirping, and an occasional bark from a chipmunk. This is the ideal place to forget about life in the big city, with the horns honking, the sirens in the middle of the night, and the slamming of doors back at the dorm.

Chase has by this time, settled down somewhat, and he is hoping that they can do some fishing in the morning, as Joseph has told them that a small river is not far away.

However, Joseph reminds them, "There are bears and even mountain lions around here, so always carry a gun, and don't let your guard down, and be aware of your surroundings. Also", he cautions, "to never travel alone, always go with someone. People have gone into these woods and have never come out."

He glances over at Chase and says, "No, not from having been attacked by a monster, but they made a big mistake and wondered off by themselves, and became lost, they would walk until they starved to death. This area is that big," Joseph looks seriously at his two friends and tells them, "so don't get careless."

Ethan and Chase understand what Joseph is telling them, and they both agree to what he said.

The next few days are very relaxing for these three college students, and they even eat the fish they catch.

Feeling the urge to do some exploring, the three of them decide to hike to a small set of hills not far away. Joseph informs them, "From the hilltop, we will have a good view of the surrounding area."

After traveling for about an hour and a half, they are spotting so much wild life that Ethan tells the others, "I need to go back to the camp and get my camera, I'll be right back."

Joseph speaks up saying, "Chase and I will be waiting right here, remember to stay on the path, don't wonder off and get lost."

Giving him a quick smile, Ethan assures him, "I will go straight to the camp and back, no side trips I promise."

Ethan is very excited about the animals he has seen, and he runs the whole way back to the camp, which must be almost four miles. When he arrives back at the camp, and after catching his breath, he at once notices that something isn't right. Looking over at his tent, he can see the tent flap is open, it has been unzipped, and the snaps at the bottom are undone. Ethan knows that all the tents were zipped shut before they left, with Joseph telling them that raccoons and bears like to raid campsites.

A bear, he knows, wouldn't be so neat and careful; it would have clawed its way into the tent, shredding everything. This tells him that someone has visited their camp, and they were probably watching us and waiting until we left. Ethan now believes, that as soon as they all left, that someone came into their camp to steal their stuff. Looking beside his tent, he can see his backpack, with its contents being strewn about all over the ground. He now looks closer and sees his wallet lying nearby; Ethan knows he has seventy-eight dollars in it, along with his credit cards. Realizing at that moment, that it looks like he has just been robbed, he begins cursing. He is hoping that maybe this thief at least left his pictures and drivers license. Picking up his wallet, he's startled to see that not only are the credit cards still in it, but his money is also here. This didn't make any sense, he thought, who would go through my backpack, and remove my wallet and not take anything from it, he asks himself. This is very odd, and the only thing missing is the couple of power bars he had stuffed in the bottom of the backpack.

The other tents are untouched; scratching his head, Ethan now puts his things back into his backpack.

He gets his camera, and as he is looking around, a strange feeling now comes over him. It is a sensation that tells him that someone is watching him at this very moment. He quickly pulls his rifle from his shoulder, checking once to make sure it is loaded. With a watchful eye, he now begins slowly walking the perimeter of the camp. Carefully placing each footstep, the woods now seem different somehow, but he can't put his finger on just why they appear this way.

Too much talk about legendary creatures and Shadow Beasts, it has put him on edge. He knows none of those stories are true, but nonetheless Ethan has a sixth sense of being watched. With the rifle pointed at the woods, his heavy breathing causes the end of the barrel to go up and down. After he makes a full circle around the camp, he waits patiently for a moment. Finally not seeing or hearing anything unusual, he now hurries back down the path to join his friends.

Unknown to Ethan, a set of cold eyes watches him from deep in the forest, as he makes his way down the path. This creature of folklore and mystery now silently moves in Ethan's direction, and it travels as if it floating over the ground, not making a sound.

After going down the path only a short distance, Ethan is once again getting that strange feeling that someone is watching him. He stops several times to look behind him, but he can see nothing. He feels a presence that he can't explain, and the hair on the back of his neck stands up. After rounding a sharp bend in the path, he decides to climb quickly up a nearby tree. Here he will wait, and he hopes, that he can catch whomever, or whatever is following him. He knows mountain lions live in this area, and they are very stealthy. He brings his rifle up to his shoulder, placing a finger on the trigger he now patently waits.

A few minutes pass, without seeing or hearing anything, he begins to have doubts. Thinking that maybe it is just his imagination. However, just as he is about to climb down, something catches his eye; it's a slight movement not far away. Ethan now presses himself tightly against the tree, his heart is now beating faster, and he is breathing out of his mouth as if he were in a race. The wait is nerve racking, and another ten minutes passes and nothing, the woods are silent. Ethan now puts his rifle back onto his shoulder and begins to climb down, but once on the ground he sees a thick patch of bushes move. "Now," he says to himself, "whomever or whatever you are I got you in my sights."

Gritting his teeth, and taking careful aim Ethan pulls the hammer back on his rifle; his hands at this time are starting to shake.

Just as he starts to yell, in an attempt to force this unknown something out into the open, a porcupine comes waddling out. Ethan almost pulls the trigger, and a smile crosses his face, shaking his head as he turns to walk away. Still thinking about the porcupine, he suddenly hears a great crashing sound very close to his left.

Startled and nearly falling down, he brings his rifle up and in the distance; he can see a large dark figure running away. Now frozen in his steps, Ethan knows what he is seeing is no bear. The creature must stand at least eight feet tall, and has long arms that move by its sides as it runs. That awful smell is again in the air, and a very confused Ethan remains motionless until the creature is out of sight.

After several minutes, he now realizes that his shirt is wet, he has broken out into a cold sweat. Now for a very long time, he keeps the rifle pointed in the direction that he last saw the dark figure. After finally calming down, he gets quickly back on the path and continues in the direction that will lead him to his friends. Ethan, without realizing it is now running down the path, every minute to him seems to take ten times that long. Finally, he meets his friends as they are coming up the path. Out of breath, and excited, Ethan tries explaining what has just happened to him. Joseph at this point is not worried about the things his friends say they have seen. He has lived in the woods his whole life, and not once has he seen anything remotely close to what his two friends are describing. "These are creatures that are only in the crazy stories that my Grandfather made up," Joseph tells Ethan and Chase.

Upset and agitated, Ethan grabs a hold of Joseph by the arm telling him in an angry voice, "I know what I saw, it was not a bear, and so don't tell me it was a bear!"

Surprised by this show of emotion, "Very well," replies Joseph, "just calm down, lets think about this."

These are guys that grew up in the city, Joseph knows, and he figures that they are a little more afraid of the woods than they have let on. Nonetheless, this latest incident has put all three on the alert.

"We'll go back to the camp," suggests Joseph, "then we'll decide what to do next."

This idea gets no argument from Chase, and the three walk close together back up the path.

Once back at their camp, the tents are inspected, and everything seems in its place.

Ethan again tells them as he points to the ground, "My backpack and it contents were scattered on the ground and my tent flaps were undone."

Not seeing anything out of place, Chase remarks, "They look okay to me."

Throwing his hands in the air, "Of course they do now," angrily replies Ethan, "I told you I put everything back before leaving."

Joseph knows that his friend Ethan isn't the type of person to exaggerate a story, so he walks into the woods and circles around the camp. After awhile Joseph walks back into camp and over by Ethan, he tells him, "I did see signs that something large had been moving around in the thick bushes, it could have been a bear."

Shaking his head, "No" answers Ethan, "It was no bear, you have to believe me."

Joseph puts his hand on Ethan's shoulder saying, "I believe you my friend."

They agree that at night they will each take turns staying awake.

As night approaches, they build up the fire. Keenly keeping a careful watch on their surroundings, none of three has much to say before they turn in for the night. They listen as the wind rustles through the treetops, and they watch as the burning embers from the fire flicker skyward.

On Josephs watch, he suddenly becomes aware of a foul smell in the air, grabbing his rifle he scans the darkness. He can recall his grandfather telling him of the terrible smell that is always present when a Shadow Beast is around. Joseph again laughs this off, and instead he tells himself that this smell is nothing more than a skunk. However, he constantly searches the darkness, and again he gets a strange feeling. He repeats to himself that there is nothing in these woods to be afraid of, and there certainly isn't any mythical beast.

However, young Joseph Browndeer knows that being a Native American that it is in his blood to believe in the spirit world, and of supernatural beings. Yet he has tried to break away from this, to live outside the beliefs of his people. He now searches his soul for answers, trying to put the sacred stories out of his mind. He battles against his Native ancestry, their belief in the spirit world and the after life. He knows he must one day make this decision, and at this point in his life he is scared and unsure. As much as he tries to think and act like the white man, he keeps finding himself drawn back to his native roots. His people live a simple and uncomplicated life, why would they want to change. Maybe his ambitions to be different are unfounded; maybe they show how insecure he is. Whatever the reason, young Joseph Browndeer has some tough and trying decisions to make. He struggles with this dilemma the rest of the night, and yet has not come to a conclusion as to which way he should go.

The morning sun comes up, and the long night ends without incidence.

It is now early morning and Ethan tells Joseph, "I want to do some exploring, but I don't want to go alone." He looks over at Chase, and asks, "Want to come along?"

Chase however has declined the offer to go along, saying, "I have seen all the wild life I want to see, I'm staying right here."

Joseph tries talking his friend out of this, telling him, "You know it is dangerous to be alone in these woods. If you become hurt and injured, we may never find you."

Ethan replies, "I promise you that I will be very careful and that I won't go far."

Joseph reminds him, "You should stay close to the river, that way you won't get lost. And it will make finding you easier." Joseph too has decided to stay in camp, and he and Chase will wait for Ethan to return.

Alone, but feeling confident, Ethan now makes his way north along a small shallow creek. It has many large rocks showing above the water, making it easy to cross without getting wet. Ethan has traveled about three miles from the camp, stopping occasionally to familiarize himself with the area. After following the creek for several more miles, he spots a mother elk with her calf. Excited, he decides to follow them and to see just how close he can get to them before they notice him. He watches as the two elk slowly make their way down stream and when the mother elk would turn her head in his direction, he did his best at hiding behind trees and large boulders. Soon he watches as the two elk go up the creek bank, and into the forest, and they are soon lost from sight. He now hurries to the place that the elk have entered the woods and he follows their tracks a short distance. The forest floor here is thick with leaves and pine needles; it now becomes impossible to see which way they went.

Unknown to Ethan a cold set of eyes are now watching him, it sees him leave the creek and enter the woods.

Ethan has forgotten about the previous day's strange encounter and he leisurely steps farther into the woods when suddenly he gets wind of a bad smell, as if something is dead nearby. His first thought is hoping that this dead animal doesn't attract bears to this area. He also doesn't want to get to far from the creek, remembering what Joseph had told him. Ethan has now gone just a little farther into the woods when he is about to give up and return to camp, that is when something catches his eye. Not more than twenty yards away he spots a small group of pine trees move, "so this" he whispers, "is where the mother elk has taken her calf." With all this cover, he knows he can get quite close to the elk before they spot him. Therefore, he bends down to go under the branches of a large tree when he hears a strange sound, "Whoop Whoop."

He can tell that it isn't coming from the two elks, and he is sure a bear or lion hadn't made it. Thinking for a moment, that maybe he should turn around and start heading for camp. However, his curiosity gets the better of him and he just has to see what this animal is. His 30-30 rifle slung over his shoulder gives him the extra encouragement that he needs. Ethan moves several yards closer, and he kneels down and while looking under the branches of a large pine tree, he is startled to see a pair of legs about fifteen yards away. It is odd to him, that whoever this person is would be wearing fur boots and fur pants, when it's not even cold. Curious to find out who this is, Ethan yells to him, "Who are you, and why are you following me?"

Instantly this man turns away from Ethan and begins running in the opposite direction very quickly. All Ethan sees is this persons legs, but it is evident by the sound of his feet hitting the ground that this is a rather large man. Ethan scratches his head at why someone would not answer him when he called out to him. What are they afraid of he wonders?

The mother elk and her calf have also been spooked by this, and they move very quickly away.

When he begins making his way back to the creek he finds a set of large foot prints. They are human he can see, but much larger than any he has ever seen before. Ethan wears a size 12 shoe and these tracks have to be at least five inches longer than his. As he looks closer, he can see this person's footprint goes three fourths of an inch into the ground. Ethan steps next to it and his shoe print only goes in about a quarter of an inch. He weighs 185 pounds, so who or whatever made these tracks, he knows must weigh close to six hundred pounds. "If it is a man," he asks himself, "than how can someone weighing so much be able to run as swiftly as he did?"

His next question is, "and why is this person out here in their bare feet," it just didn't make any sense. Looking again at the tracks, "this is one big something," Ethan says, he will let Joseph know what he's seen when he gets back to the camp.

Going a little farther Ethan is startled as he is walking back to the creek that these large tracks are right alongside his earlier tracks, meaning this other man was following him, this puts him on edge.

Getting closer to the small creek, Ethan hears a loud splash. Now with his heart racing, he hurries through the woods and is soon standing on the ridge overlooking the creek; he can see large waves hitting the shore. He knows something very big caused this, however looking in all directions he is unable to spot what animal was just here. Ethan now carries his rifle close to his side, with his finger on the trigger. He isn't going to run, instead he moves cautiously along the path, keeping a sharp eye on his surroundings like Joseph had told him to do. The few miles back to camp take longer than he wanted.

When he finally arrives back at the camp, he sees that both Joseph and Chase are gathering firewood. Ethan calls them over, "You guys aren't going to believe what happened to me."

Looking up and smiling, "Let me guess," answers Joseph, "you took so many pictures that you ran out of film."

"I wish that were it," replies Ethan, "I saw a large man wearing fur boots, and he moved very quickly."

Now curious Joseph needs to hear more, "What did the man look like?"

Wiping the sweat from his face and after getting a drink, "I only saw his legs," answers Ethan, "but he was really big."

Chase thinks his friend is only saying this to scare him, "If you're lying, I swear I'll through you in that creek."

Shaking his head, "No, I'm not lying, and I also found large footprints and they were bigger than mine."

Thinking about this for a second, Joseph says, "Nothing I know of can make a track like that, and as for that person you saw running, he must be out here to scare us away."

With a dismayed reaction, Chase looks at Ethan and says, "You know what I saw a few days ago on our way here must have been that same person." He goes on and says, "The disguise looked very real to me, the people that don't want us here are sure going out of their way to scare us."

Not liking this at all, "Yes," replies Joseph, "who knows what they will try next."

Nevertheless, Ethan has to ask, "Just how was this person able to put those footprints so deep into the ground?"

Confused by all of this, Joseph shakes his head and says, "I don't know, but I'm sure it's just a trick."

Now as dusk settles over the forest, the three friends relax as they are sitting around the fire discussing the upcoming school year. They hear the usual sounds of the forest, with the constant buzz of the insects, the night howls hoot echoing through the forest, and in the distance, they can hear the wolves begin their night songs. The three are laughing and telling jokes, when Chase suddenly speaks up, and looking around, he asks, "What happened to the noise?"

The three are now quiet; a serious look is on their faces.

Taking a glance around, "He is right," says Joseph, "the forest has gone silent."

With a look of confusion on their faces, they try to figure out why the noise from the animals has suddenly stopped. It is an eerie silence and Ethan reaches over and grabs his rifle. The three young men are again startled when they hear a loud crashing sound not far from their camp. The sound of tree branches breaking and heavy footsteps echoes through the forest. Each now jumps up and grabs his rifle and with their flashlights shining into the forest. They strain their eyes trying to catch a glimpse of what caused the noise. After a moment, Chase gets very excited and yells, "I saw a shadow walking in the woods!"

With their hearts beating faster, each has his finger on the trigger of his rifle.

Waving his rifle around, "Okay," demands Chase in a shaky voice, "now tell me what that was?"

Before anyone can answer, Chase points his rifle at the woods and shouts, "Maybe if I fire a few rounds into the woods maybe that will scare this person away."

Reaching over, Ethan very quickly grabs Chase's rifle by the barrel and looks him in the eyes, and says, "Don't be foolish, if it is just a person out there trying to scare us and you shoot him, you will go to jail."

Thinking for a moment, Chase looks at his friend and says, "Your right, we don't want to hurt anyone."

Trying to calm his friends down, Joseph speaks up saying, "Maybe it's a bear, as they do sometimes knock down old trees to get at the honey in a bee hive."

Ethan agrees and says, "That's probably all it is." He puts his hand on Chases shoulder, and with a wink says, "Don't let the sounds of the forest scare you."

After a few minutes the three now sit back down and stare at the fire. However, just as they begin talking again, a rock lands on the ground in front of them. Startled and alarmed yet again, the three quickly stand back up, with Chase demanding; "Now I know that bears can't throw rocks!"

Running out of ideas, "Than it must be that person you saw earlier," A flabbergasted Joseph insists.

Ethan speaks up asking, "Are you telling me that someone is out here in the middle of nowhere, in the middle of the night, with no flashlight, and he's throwing rocks at us?"

Trying his best to come up with logical answers, "It has to be," replies Joseph with a nervous tone to his words, "what else could it be?"

Again, a cold set of eyes watches the three young men from deep in the woods.

The three stand very close to each other, Ethan now looks at Joseph and says, "Remember the story your grandfather told us about the large creature that guards the forest, he said that the creatures would sometimes throw rocks."

Getting agitated, "That is total nonsense," replies Joseph with a hint of resentment, "No such creature exists. My Grandfather made up those dumb stories, none of them are true."

Ethan answers back, "The other tribal leaders also spoke of these large ape like creatures that live in these woods, what about their stories?"

"Just stories," answers Joseph hastily, "I'll prove to you that it is just a person in a gorilla suit that is out here trying to scare us."

With a concerned expression on his face and gripping his rifle tightly, "And how do you think you can do that?" asks Chase.

After setting his rifle down, "Tomorrow," replies Joseph, "We'll set a trap; I know many ways to catch this prankster."

The tension is very high in the camp, and Chase suggests, "I think that again tonight we should take turns staying up and keeping watch, no telling what this person might do."

It is agreed, and each takes their turn staying awake while the others sleep.

However, given the strange things that are happening to them, it is impossible for any of them to sleep. As they keep a close eye on their surroundings, the rest of the night ends without another incident.

When morning comes, they are in a good mood, despite what has happened. They gather the supplies that they will need, and going into the woods, they set several traps in the hope of catching this person that has been harassing them. Joseph proves very knowledgeable about building traps and they build three such traps. Only these traps are much bigger than the ones he used to catch rabbits and other small game. Using nearby trees and the rope they brought with them, the traps are big enough and strong enough to easily lift a man off his feet and suspend him in the air. To test his traps, Chase and Ethan both volunteer, and they walk into the trip rope and the ropes lying on the ground that are concealed under leaves suddenly spring into action. Before either Chase or Ethan knows what has happened, both are quickly lifted up into the air, and they are now hanging upside down. The three of them start to laugh; "This is going to be a lot of fun," Ethan tells the others, "I can't wait to see the look on that guys face when he is hanging upside down."

After lowering them to the ground, Joseph resets the trap and the three go back to their camp.

The rest of the day is quiet, as each take their turn getting some sleep. At supper that evening, Joseph prepares cooked squirrel. It is something that Ethan has never tried before, and by the look on Chases face, that it must be his first taste of squirrel too.

While putting the meat on their plates, Joseph says, "I checked the traps earlier and still nothing."

"Don't worry," Ethan replies, "this person usually comes around after dark."

Chase is surprised that he finds the cooked squirrel quit tasty, and remarks, "Tastes a little like chicken, I'll have to remember this."

As the three build up the fire and the sky turns dark, a look of nervousness is on their faces.

Each one is now in his own thoughts, apprehensive and somewhat worried about this person that seems to be stalking them.

Ethan speaks up asking, "So what do we do with this person when we catch him?"

Chase quickly responds by saying, "We should just leave him hang out there for several hours, and let him know that scaring people is wrong."

Disagreeing with that, Ethan looks over at Joseph who says, "I guess I never thought of that, we can't leave him hanging from that tree forever, I suppose we'll get his name and then let him go. On our way back home we can stop at the local police station and let them know what this person has been up to, let them deal with him."

Thinking about this, the others agree that this is probably the best thing to do.

Around 10 p.m. when they are about to turn in for the night a foul smell fills the air, this causes each of them to stop what they are doing. They stare at one another, as they know that this foul smell is somehow connected to the person who is out here playing jokes on them.

Motioning with his hands, Joseph quietly tells the others, "Just stay calm, don't get up and walk around, we want this person to think that we don't know he's out there."

The three remain silent, listening for the slightest sound that will give them a clue to just where this person is.

As the minutes tick by, and the foul smell increases, the three nervously wait. Biting his lip, Chase begins tapping his foot on the ground. Ethan also is uncomfortable with this waiting. He begins to grind his teeth, his fists clinched so tight that his knuckles turn white. Joseph is sitting with his eyes closed, concentrating on the sounds around them.

Then out of the dark woods, they can hear a crashing sound, and it's coming from the direction of one of the traps. The three now spring to their feet and with Chase the only one grabbing his gun, Ethan and Joseph both grab their flashlights instead. Excited as they make their way into the woods, they jostle for position, each wanting to be in the lead. They momentarily stop as they can hear the sound of tree limbs breaking. This is followed by a terrible crashing sound, as if something has fallen out of a tree. Next, a howling noise that sends chills up their spines has them standing very close to each other. With blank stares on their faces, each looks at the other, no one is saying a word. Slowly they again proceed down the narrow path towards the trap. From a distance of thirty feet, they can see that indeed something is in their trap.

The three now inch ever closer, with Chase being the only one to bring his rifle they push him out in front. Their flashlights shining ahead, trying to penetrate the darkness to reveal what they have caught. Their hearts stop beating when they see that whatever it is that is in the trap has now fallen to the ground. They see just a large shadow and watch in total fright as this thing stands up on two legs and lets out a deafening sound that has the three young men frozen with fear. Standing so close to each other, they can feel the other shaking. Their flashlights can only make out the image of what has just broken out of the trap.

Trying to control his breathing, Joseph says in a shaky voice, "No man could have escaped this trap."

Finally able to speak, "If it is not a man, then what in the hell is that thing," asks Ethan?

Joseph doesn't answer, his muscles tight with fear, all he can do is put his hand over his mouth.

Chase is trying to point his rifle at it, but his hands are shaking so badly that he has to hand it over to Ethan. Ethan knows that this puny rifle would not kill this huge beast, it probably wouldn't even slow it down if it came charging at them.

As the three slowly begin to back up, sliding their feet across the ground, the creature slams its fists down onto the ground causing the earth beneath their feet to vibrate. This is all the three young men needed and they turn and run as fast as they can back to the camp. Ethan and Joseph both grab their rifles and stand terrified at what has just happened.

All three are pointing their rifles at the woods, anticipating at any moment that this creature will come bursting out.

After several minutes of silence, Joseph speaks up saying, "I never believed the stories my Grandfather told me about the Shadow Beasts. I think that maybe I should have paid more attention, because there's no denying what we just saw."

Ethan now standing very close to Joseph, and not taking his eyes off the woods asks, "So if this is a Shadow Beast, what do we do?"

"Nothing," answers Joseph in a unsteady voice, "as long as we don't hurt any of them we will be safe, they are just curious and only want to watch us, nothing more."

Quickly throwing all of their wood onto the fire trying to build it up as high as they can, hoping this will keep the creature away. After nervously watching the woods for nearly an hour, and hearing no more sounds, they begin to relax. The three scared young men now sit around their fire and try to understand how a creature so large could have managed to elude hunters and photographers for all these years.

Ethan remarks, "Kicking Bear had mentioned how these so called Guardians of The Forest, are able to blend in with their surroundings so well that one standing only a few feet away could go undetected. Almost like a chameleon, able to change its color to match its surroundings."

Still visibly shaken, Joseph states, "My grandfather also said that this mystical beast could change its shape and take the form of a tree or a rock. However, that part of his story is total nonsense." He looks at his two companions and smiles, "At least I hope that part of his story is nonsense."

Scratching their heads at this unbelievable turn of events, the three must come to grips with reality. What they saw was indeed a living, breathing creature. There was no more assuming and hoping that it was just a man in a gorilla suit out to scare them. This mythical creature, part folklore, part superstition, but very real, is something they will never forget.

The heat from the fire causes them to back up, ever weary of their distance from the trees. The three now discuss all the possibilities for the existence of this creature.

Taking a deep breath, Ethan speaks up, "This may be a long shot, but i believe that it is an unknown species of ape, like a gorilla, that somehow has managed to live here. Where it came from and how it got here I don't have a clue."

Still bewildered, Joseph lowers his head; trying to come to grips with a story that he has steadfastly rejected his whole life.

Putting his hands together as he looks up with a blank stare, Joseph comments, "I can't believe how blind I have been. To have ignored my own people, with their beliefs and their traditions, it saddens me. My grandfather must be very disappointed in me."

"You went with what you thought was the right path," says Ethan, "there is nothing wrong with wanting to be independent. Your grandfather is a wise man, he knows your spirit is strong, and he believes in you."

Taking comfort in those words he looks at his friend, "Did my grandfather really say that he believes in me?"

Smiling and nodding his head, "Your grandfather said that you remind him a lot of himself when he was your age. He worries that you will be just as headstrong and stubborn, just like he was. That you will have to do things your own way, and he admires that in you."

Now holding his chin up, Joseph looks at the night sky. Without looking away he says, "Thank you Ethan, not only for being my friend, but also for listening to my grandfather."

Ethan gives him a slap on the back, "I think when we get back to your reservation, we need to sit down with your grandfather, as there are a few questions I'd like to ask him."

"Yes my friend, there are many questions that need answers. But first I owe my grandfather an apology, and to ask for his forgiveness."

As Ethan is about to speak, Chase interrupts, "I have a theory about that creature and where it came from."

Quickly getting their attention, they both turn their heads towards Chase.

"You may think I'm nuts, but I think that creature is an alien from space."

This gets the two to start laughing, despite the seriousness of the situation.

"You are way off base with that idea," a still laughing Ethan replies.

Not appreciating their lack of confidence in him, "I'm serious guys, it could be an alien, they exist you know."

Several quiet minutes pass before the three get serious again. The look on their faces, with the wrinkled forehead and terse lips, reveal just how apprehensive and concerned they really are.

With a solemn look, Joseph now stands up, "My people," he starts out, "have known about these creatures for many centuries, they appear in all the ancient stories."

Closing his eyes, "We have seen the sacred beast; I pray that it was not a bad omen."

After hearing this, a worried Chase asks, "What should we do now?"

After discussing the situation for a while; it is agreed, that they will pack up their things and leave the next day. This bizarre incident has put an end to their relaxed trip in the great outdoors.

With the campfire burning brightly, giving them a small of measure of security, "What a story we have to tell when we get back," Chase utters, "and we haven't even been drinking."

The three laugh; as it will indeed be quit a tall tale, they realize that no one is going to believe them.

Soon the tension in the air begins to fade, and they all seem a little more relaxed and at ease.

While the three are lying on the ground next to the fire, Ethan throws a stick hitting Chase in the arm.

Confused, Chase immediately demands, "What did you do that for?"

With a chuckle, Ethan replies, "Aliens from space, are you serious?"

Smiling, Chase looks around saying, "What's wrong with that theory?"

The three now begin to laugh, and Ethan says, "You watch the skies, I'm watching the woods." After a few more jokes, the laughing subsides and the three settle down for the night.

In the morning, after another sleepless night, Ethan and Joseph cautiously go into the woods and examine the trap that had temporally held this creature. When they reach the trap, they can see how the rope has been broken as if it were nothing more than a piece of string. The small trees that are nearby are also broken, and they are lying on the ground as if run over by a bulldozer.

The two know by their quick examination, that this creature must have great strength. They aren't sure if their rifles will be able to stop this thing if they had to. Looking around, they can see many large tracks are on the ground, and they now get the feeling right then that they are being watched. Standing perfectly still, trying to see into the dense forest for any movement that might give away the location of this beast.

Motioning with his hands, "We will leave everything as it is," Joseph says, "I will bring others from my tribe here so they to can see the power of this beast."

Ethan is about to say something when they hear several gunshots. Standing perfectly still, they know these gunshots are coming from their camp. Turning around they hurry as fast as they can back towards the camp. As they emerge from the forest and into the clearing, they see Chase pointing at a bush nearby, yelling, "I just shot a bear."

Ethan and Joseph, their rifles at the ready, now nervously go over to where Chase is pointing. With his gun barrel shaking, Chase takes a few steps backwards. Getting on each side of their friend, the two cautiously look beyond the bush. To their surprise, nothing is there, the bear is gone, but there is much blood on the ground.

Investigating closer, Joseph remarks, "By the blood on the ground, this bear is only wounded, and it has now run into the forest."

They must decide weather to leave right now as planned, or follow this wounded bear. Following the blood trail with his eyes, Joseph sees that it leads deep into the woods. At this point Chase speaks up saying, "Just forget about it, the bear will go somewhere and die."

Displeased after hearing his friend say this, "No" replies Joseph sternly, "We cannot let a wounded animal suffer, we will find it and end its suffering."

Not wanting to go any farther, Chase tells them, "I don't like being out in these woods, so I'm going to stay back at the camp."

An argument now follows between him and Joseph over what is the right thing to do.

Joseph demands, "You should be the one to end this bears suffering, sense you are the one that shot it."

Shaking his head, Chase replies, "I'm not good at those things; one of you will have to do it"

Waving his hand back and forth, "Doesn't matter," argues Joseph, "you have a responsibility, now follow me."

Taking a step back, "No way, I'm not going any farther."

"You will do what is right, and you will do it now!"

As Joseph and Chase move closer and begin to stare at one another, Ethan finally steps in, and tells Chase, "You go back to the camp and start packing. I and Joseph will find this wounded bear and take care of it, and we will be back as soon as we can and then we can all leave."

Angry, Joseph isn't happy about this, but Ethan grabs him by the arm and pulls him down the path.

"We can't waste time arguing," declares Ethan, "what is done is done."

The two now pick up the blood trail and continue following it, soon it becomes apparent to Joseph that this might not be a bear.

Joseph says to Ethan, "The trail in which this wounded animal is going is not what a bear would do."

Puzzled, "What are you saying," asks Ethan?

"A wounded bear," replies Joseph, "Would look for a cave or a downed tree and try to hide in it, yet, this animal is running towards the mountains."

Starting to get an uneasy feeling, "So what are we trailing," asks Ethan, "If it's not a bear that Chase says he shot."

Looking around, obviously uncomfortable, as he scans the woods, "I'm not sure," replies Joseph, "Let's continue following it and find out."

The two have now gone much deeper into the forest than they had planned on. Having left the security of the path to follow the blood trail, it has taken them into unfamiliar surroundings. Ethan by now is lost, but he has confidence in Joseph that he can find the right trail back to their campsite.

Stopping abruptly, Joseph suddenly grabs Ethan by the arm and says, "We are not alone out here, I have a strange feeling of being watched."

Both men stand perfectly still as they stare intensely into the thick canopy of trees and bushes. The forest has gone silent, not a chirp, not a howl, nothing. Moving into a defensive posture, the two stand back to back.

"I know something is out here watching us," whispers Joseph, "and its no bear or mountain lion."

"If it's the Shadow Beast," utters Ethan, "why should we be afraid, we have done no harm to it."

"I just have a bad feeling," answers Joseph, "I can't explain it."

At this point, the two have decided that they should turn around now, and head back to the camp.

"We need to get out of these woods," a nervous Joseph says, "something isn't right."

Hearing the fear in his friend's voice that he has not heard before, Ethan is more than happy to get out of these woods.

The two are indeed being watched, and silently followed, by a very large creature, as it moves through the brush.

As they are walking back towards the camp, a faint noise catches their attention. The two pull up their rifles, and begin scanning the area quickly, their hearts now beating faster.

They can see no movement, and a moment later, they again hear a faint noise.

Without saying a word, the two walk a short distance in the direction of the noise. Soon they leave the forest and find themselves on a rocky ledge looking down into a small raven. There, lying at the bottom they see what looks like a monkey. Surprised, both young men know that there are no wild monkeys in this state or even in the whole country. After staring at this animal for a moment, they both try to come up with an explanation for this monkey being out here in these woods. Scratching their heads, this sight has both young men stumped.

When to their surprise they suddenly observe this monkey begin to move, and then it turns itself over. Moving closer to the edge to get a better look at it, they are both shocked by the almost human like face on this monkey.

With a frightened look on his face, catching his breath, Joseph backs as he covers his mouth.

"What is wrong, what do you see?"

Stuttering in a panicky voice, "That is no monkey," he points with a shaking finger, "it's a young Shadow Beast."

Wide eyed after hearing this, Ethan leans forward to get a better look down into the raven. Joseph grabs him by the shoulder and tells him firmly, "We must leave these woods right now."

Ethan is hesitant; he doesn't understand why they need to hurry off so quickly. Joseph looks him right in the eyes and says, "What Chase shot back at the camp was no bear, it was a Shadow Beast, and now these creatures will be coming to get revenge. Don't you remember what my grandfather said about if anyone hurts one of them, that they will seek revenge."

His face lighting up, Ethan now understands the urgency in Joseph's voice. Both turn to run when the surrounding woods seem to come alive with movement. Whistling and grunts can now be heard everywhere, letting them know that indeed they are not alone. With the trail leading back to their camp blocked, Joseph looks around for another possible escape route. With no other option, their only chance of escape is to scale down into a nearby steep gorge. Without wasting any more time, the two now move fast and begin climbing down towards the gorge. As they are halfway down the hillside, rocks begin to fall all around them. It is apparent to them now that other Shadow Beasts are very close by.

Joseph and Ethan manage to make it to the bottom of the gorge, despite sometimes slipping and rolling part of the way. They get to their feet quickly and hurry between the narrows steep banks that rise up sharply on both sides.

With Joseph calling, "Just keep running and don't look back!"

The two run in silence, only mere inches separate the two as their strides and arm swings match each other perfectly. Their hearts sink when the gorge comes to an abrupt end. Now the two find themselves standing on a protrusion a hundred feet from the ground below.

The two stop to catch their breath, and unable to go back they way they have just come, Ethan gets down on one knee and points his rifle up the gorge.

Wiping the sweat from his forehead, "It looks like we can't go any further; we'll have to fight the Shadow Beasts here."

A confrontation with these beasts is not what Joseph wants, so he desperately looks around for a way out.

About to give up and join his friend, Joseph spots what could be an escape route.

Tapping his friend on the shoulder, Joseph points to a small ledge leading across the face of a cliff.

"I think we can manage to make it on that ledge, it's better than trying to fight them here."

Giving it long hard look, Ethan replies, "That is a very small ledge and it's a long ways to the bottom."

Doing his best to be brave, "We can make it, just trust me and don't look down."

Taking a couple deep breaths, Ethan slaps Joseph on the back, "I trust you, if you think we can make it, than lets go."

With Joseph in the lead, the two must press their body close to the rock wall, sliding their feet carefully across the ground. Ever so slowly, they make their way over to where the ledge widens out. Here the ledge ends, and now they are forced to climb down the cliff to another ledge about ten feet below them. While managing their way across the face of this mountain, they can hear that something is just above them. The Shadow Beast now stands on the rim of the cliff just above Joseph and Ethan. It is grunting and beating the ground with its fists, causing rocks and dirt to fall over the edge and onto the two men below.

Joseph knows that if all the stories his Grandfather has told him are true, then it is unlikely that any of them will make it back home alive. The Shadow Beasts are masters of the forest; they know every tree, every valley, it will be impossible to hide from them. The two still have their rifles, and that at least does give them some measure of hope.

CHAPTER 4

Once he gets back to the camp, Chase begins packing up his stuff; he tries his cell phone again but still no reception. Wanting to forget this trip, and get back to civilization as soon as possible.

Still agitated by his near fight with Joseph, Chase has lowered his guard. He curses as he puts stuff into his backpack, oblivious to anything around him. A rustling of the brush nearby gets his attention, thinking it is his friends returning he calls out, "Did you find that bear?"

He gets an uneasy feeling when he gets no answer. Looking over, Chase can see his rifle on the far side of the camp; it is leaning against a tree. He is now getting a strange feeling, as if someone is watching him. Looking around and not seeing anyone, he now begins walking towards his rifle, not wanting to take any chances. A loud rustling of the brush from behind startles him, causing him to stop and turn around. What he sees stepping out of the forest is like something out of a nightmare. Stunned, mouth agape and eyes wide open, he sees a very big fur covered animal standing upright on two legs. Its arms hang down to its knees and its massive head seems to sit right on its shoulders as if it has no neck. The face is flat, hairless and with a protruding brow; and the site of those enormous teeth sends a shiver through his body. Chase is trying to catch his breath, startled he takes several steps back at the sight of this monster, only to trip and fall. Panic stricken, he begins franticly crawling towards his rifle, looking back only to see this huge hairy creature getting closer, he is so scared that he is unable to yell. He now shuffles across the ground in a clumsy way, and when he is about to grab his rifle something with very large hands grabs him forcibly by the leg and picks him straight up into the air.

Chase, hanging upside down, is now face to face with this monster and he is now shaking uncontrollably. Trying his best to get away, but the creature now bares its teeth and lets out a deafening roar. All Chase can do is to put his hands over his ears, close his eyes and pray for a miracle. To his surprise, the beast lets go its grip and he drops to the ground. Once on the ground he starts to roll away, hoping to make it to his rifle. However, once again, he feels a large hand grab his leg; the creature drags Chase across the ground like a rag doll. Chase is trying to catch his breath as he desperately grabs at the ground in an attempt to stop himself. He manages to turn onto his back, and grabbing a baseball size rock he throws it at the beast, striking it in the back of the head. The beast now releases its grip, and Chase thinking he has won his freedom, now springs to his knees, and he begins crawling away quickly. However, a pair of huge hands reaches for him, one grabbing his shoulder, the other his hip. Chase now screams out, but it does no good, as he is lifted effortlessly high into the air. The beast shakes him violently; next, it throws Chase through the air, where he lands on one of the tents.

The force of him landing on the tent causes it to collapse to the ground. Laying there dazed and hurting, Chase can see through blurred vision that the beast is coming towards him again. With all his strength, he manages to stumble to his feet, knowing now that escape is impossible. Without thinking, Chase charges straight at the beast, recalling his high school football days, where he received numerous awards for being a fierce defensive lineman.

Chase puts everything into his charge, hoping to knock the beast down and gain some time to come up with a plan of action, still hoping to make it over to his rifle. However, running into this beast, is like hitting a brick wall. Chase crumbles to the ground, now realizing how foolish his action was. While he is trying to catch his breath, he feels himself once again, being picked up by the beast. It holds him out in front to get a look at him, all the while Chase has his arms in front of his face. After a brief moment of not knowing what is going to happen next, this time the creature slams him hard against its shoulder. Chase is nauseated and bruised, and on the verge of blacking out. He is in a panic state, he again begins swinging wildly and screaming for help. The beast, with just one hand, lifts Chase high into the air, then it tosses him onto its other shoulder, and it now begins walking into the forest.

Chase is carried this way for miles, and no amount of struggling and kicking is able to loosen the beasts grip on him. As nightfall comes, the beast continues walking; not even stopping once to rest. Chase can tell that the creature is taking him up towards the mountains, as the air is now cooler than before. Lifting his head up, he can just make out other shadowy forms around him, they are only a few feet away. He can hear grunt and groan sounds, almost monkey like. This he knows are other creatures like the one carrying him. He has a knife on his belt, but to try to stab this creature will only anger it. Surrounded by these creatures, he knows his chance of escape is zero. A sickening feeling is in his stomach, and several times he nearly vomits.

By the light of the moon, he sees the entrance to a cave; "This" he believes, "is where they are going to eat me."

The huge creature ducts its head down as it goes into the cave and then stands upright again. The smell in here is awful; it reminds Chase of rotting flesh. He is taken down several tunnels and then is thrown hard to the ground, which temporarily knocks the wind out of him. As he is waiting for his eyes to adjust to the dark, he can hear heavy footsteps approaching him. Scrambling about on his hands and knees, frantically he reaches around trying to find something he can use as a weapon. He grabs what feels like a baseball bat, but upon closer examination, he realizes it is a leg bone and he quickly throws it down and backs up against the far wall.

With his heart beating fast and sweat running down his face, young Chase Watkins never imagined dying this way.

CHAPTER 5

Ethan and Joseph cautiously move farther down the cliff until they reach the bottom, from here they begin running.

Trying his best to remain calm, Joseph says, "I know where an old mining shack is located and that it might be possible to make it there before the Shadow Beasts can catch up to us."

Waving his hands, "Then let's go," yells Ethan.

Now running for their lives, they don't stop to rest or even slow down. In desperation, the two run right through several small streams, and over a rocky plain. With panic on their faces, they run through thorn bushes, which tares at their clothing and the tree branches that scratch their faces, but still they run. At one point, Joseph nearly falls off the trail and down an embankment. Acting quickly, Ethan reaches out and is able to pull him back to safety just in time. Unfortunately, Joseph's rifle has slipped out of his hand when he reached back, the rifle falls to the ground far below them. Knowing that they can't waste the time to go down and retrieve the rifle, they must continue on, hoping to outdistance the Shadow Beats.

Now the two have just the one rifle, and their slim chance of coming out of this predicament alive has just been cut in half. After clearing the forest and cresting a small hill, finally, they can see the old mining shack in the distance.

Ethan, bent 0ver and out of breath yells, "We made it, we'll be safe in there."

However, it is an open field of tall grass that they have to cross. The two must chance leaving the safety of the forest and hoping that the Shadow Beasts will not spot them. It will be very dangerous with no large boulders or trees to conceal themselves behind while they run for the old shack. Moving quickly and staying low to the ground, they stop abruptly when they spot a mother bear and her two cubs.

Putting his arm out to stop Ethan, Joseph says, "It is too dangerous to try and cross this field, the mother bear will be very protective of her cubs, she will attack as soon as she gets wind of us."

Ethan replies, "I'll fire several shots in the air to try to frighten her away."

Joseph is becoming very agitated and is constantly looking around, he knows that these Shadow Beasts can move faster than any human can, and it is important that the two get moving as soon as possible.

After firing several shots into the air, the mother bear and her two cubs begin moving away, but at a very leisure pace. After waiting several minutes, the two decide that they can't wait any longer, they have to start towards the shack now. They can't fire any more shots to try to make the bears move faster, as they need every round of ammunition they have for what might lay ahead.

The two continue walking in the tall grass and they keep one eye on the bear and the other one constantly scanning behind them, expecting at any moment that a group of those Shadow Beasts will come bursting from the forest and tear them to pieces. It is nerve racking getting so close to these bears, but they have to chance it. Now half way across the field, they watch as the mother bear has tolerated them long enough and now she turns towards the two and begins charging. Joseph and Ethan both know that it is impossible to out run this bear, so Ethan tells Joseph, "You run towards the shack and I will stay here, it should give you time to be safe." With a startled look Joseph replies, "The bear will kill you, its suicide what you're planning, I can't let you do this."

Ethan shoves his friend away saying, "There is no need for both of us to die, now go."

With that said, Joseph knows his friend is right, he looks at Ethan, and says, "Use the rifle if you have to."

After shaking hands, he reluctantly turns and runs towards the shack. Just before reaching it, he hears several shots, stopping and looking back, he is hoping to see his friend quickly following him, but he sees nothing. With a heavy heart, he goes into the old mining shack and closes the door, and then he braces it with several pieces of lumber. Joseph looks out through a small window, that is no bigger that his hand. The tall grass in the field is still, no movement, no sound. It gives him a sick feeling in his stomach. Now he is safe, but it cost a heavy price. With no food or water, and unarmed, it won't be long, and he will have to risk going back into the forest. That is, if the Shadow Beasts don't break into this old shack and extracts their revenge on him first.

However, as Joseph is looking around, his mood quickly changes when he sees a rifle lying on a small table nearby. Hoping that with this rifle, he can go back outside and help Ethan. He now springs to his feet and hurries over to the table, but his heart sinks when pulling back the bolt on the rifle he sees that it is empty, no bullets. Looking around he searches the scattered contents of this old shack, but finds nothing useful, just a shovel and an old pick axe. He knows these will be useless against the creatures that will soon be attacking this shack. He now walks back over to the door and looking out he still can see no movement. Joseph now leans his back up against the door and slowly slides down until he is sitting on the dirt floor.

With his head now in his hands, he bows forward. He keeps going over in his mind all that has occurred, and he tells himself this is like something out of a horror movie. Joseph knows that since he sees no more movement in the tall grass, and hears no more gunshots, the outcome is not good. It is now obvious to Joseph, that one of these Shadow Beasts has killed his friend Ethan. As for Chase, he has no doubt that the Shadow Beast has also killed him.

With tears beginning to run down his face, he knows it will only be a matter of time before he too will face the wrath of these creatures. His situation seems hopeless; he can see no way out. There is no one to come to his rescue, and no one to bury his body when the Shadow Beasts are finished with it. He will face death alone, and he will never see his family again. What of his grandfather, he can see him sitting in front of his little cabin smoking his pipe. Joseph would have liked to tell his grandfather that the old man was right about these Shadow Beasts, these "Guardians of The Forest," as he liked to call them. A smile crosses his face and he realizes that he should have paid more attention to the Tribal Elders. He should have learned more of their ways and listened more closely to their stories. However, it is too late now, his days are numbered, and it will take a miracle from the Great Spirit to save him. Joseph Browndeer now closes his eyes, trying desperately to recall the stories of these Shadow Beasts. Maybe there is a way to stop them, if only he could find in his soul the answer. Joseph can hear in his head, the drums from the many ceremonies that he has witnessed. How other members of his tribe believed with all their heart, the stories and myths passed down from one generation to another.

Unfortunately, not Joseph, and now he reaches deep inside his own soul, hoping to find his ancestral heritage. Praying that it's not too late, and that he will be given a chance to prove to his people that he is worthy to be called a member of the Yakama Indian Nation.

CHAPTER 6

Ethan aims his rifle at the charging bear; he does not want to shoot it. Nevertheless, if he has to he will, now taking aim he puts his finger on the trigger. Ethan is by now beginning to walk backwards, hoping to avoid firing his rifle, he isn't sure that it will stop an angry bear anyways. His foot catching a rock, Ethan suddenly trips and as he is falling back his finger pulls the trigger, by this time his rifle is pointing skyward and he misses the bear completely. However, in an instant, the bear abruptly stops and stands up on its hind legs. Its head is now looking over at the forest and with a growl; it quickly turns and runs away. Breathing a sigh of relief, Ethan thinks that another bear is nearby so he fires two more rounds hoping to scare it away also.

As he is lying on the ground a foul smell is in the air, instantly he knows now what has scared that bear away, and it wasn't the sound of his rifle, or another bear. Ethan begins crawling through the tall grass, every few minutes he raises his head up and looks around. Crawling until he is at the edge of the forest, here he stands up and looking back over the tall grass he can see the Shadow Beast coming his way. With urgency in his steps, he now begins running, it doesn't matter what direction he goes, just as long as he puts a lot of distance between him and the creature. Hoping with a little luck that he will find a large tree and in its top branches, he will be safe. However, luck is not with him, as he soon finds himself standing at the edge of a cliff. Breathing heavily and looking over he can see that the bottom is at least three hundred feet down. Now turning around he looks desperately for another way out.

Unfortunately, the Shadow Beast has caught up to him, and it is now too close and there is no going around it. Ethan now breathing heavy, and heart pounding shoulders his rifle and taking careful aim, he puts the sights right between the eyes of the beast. The creature continues walking towards Ethan and he backs up until he is now on the very edge of the cliff. Taking a glance over his shoulder, Ethan knows a fall from this height will be fatal. He turns back towards the creature, he is still hoping deep down inside that this creature is just a man in a gorilla suit. Praying that anyone in a gorilla suit that is staring down the barrel of a rifle will have known at this point that it is game over. However, and to Ethan's dismay, this creature seems not at all intimidated by his rifle.

Ethan now grits his teeth, hoping to avoid finding out if his rifle will be able to stop this beast. When suddenly the creature raises its arms into the air and it lets out a tremendous roar. Startled by this, it causes Ethan to lose his footing, and he falls back. His rifle goes flying as he desperately tries getting a grip on the rocky ledge. As hard as he tries, the lose rocks only pull away as he grabs at them, he is now in a free fall.

Ethan very quickly lands hard on his back, and has the wind knocked out of him. He lays there for a moment, slightly dazed. Looking around he now realizes that he has only fallen about ten feet or so. He is aware that he's on a very small ledge, one no bigger than he is. Thankful that he's still alive, now he must try to scale the cliff back up to the top. After cautiously getting back to his feet, a quick look down tells him that one slip and there will be no more miracles, below is nothing but a sheer cliff. Now as he is looking up, trying to figure a way up this sheer cliff, he is shocked, when a long hairy arm swings down and narrowly misses his head.

Ethan quickly drops down to his knees, and puts his hands over his head. The beast above him now begins pounding on the ground, causing rocks and dirt to fall down on him. Ethan hugs the cliff tightly, and is able to avoid being knocked off his small perch. After what seems an eternity, the pounding and screaming stops, and the debris is no longer falling all around him. He now breaths a sigh of relief, but after examining the cliff above him, it is obvious that scaling up to the top is going to be impossible. The rock surface is just too flat, there's no place to get a handhold.

CHAPTER 7

Chase lays in this dark, damp and smelly chamber all night, anticipating that at any moment he is going to be grabbed and eaten by one of these creatures. When morning does come, he is able to see somewhat by the small beams of light coming through holes in the roof of the cave. Scanning the area, he can see the room he is in measures about fifteen feet by ten feet, with the ceiling only inches away from his head when he stands up. Having not heard any sounds for quit some time, he works up the courage to walk over to the entrance to this small room. He hesitates for a moment, as he is unable to see very far in the semi darkness.

Feeling that this could be his chance to escape, he cautiously takes one-step out of the doorway. Immediately a large hairy arm hits him in the chest with such force that it knocks him back into the room and across the floor to the far wall. Chase drops to his knees clutching his ribs; he knows by the pain that several of them must be broken. A large figure now blocks the entrance, and all he can do is to pray for a miracle.

After a tense moment of starring at the beast, Chase doesn't understand why it neither attacks nor backs away. Feeling like a helpless child under its hypnotic gaze, young Chase tries not to think of what it has planned for him.

However, to his surprise he sees an old man walk past this beast and stand in front of him. Looking up surprised, Chase can see a long white beard, and the old man walks hunched over with the aid of a cane. He watches as this old man begins tapping his cane against the wall and picking at his face. Just below his left eye, Chase can see many scabs there; "It must be a nervous tic," he thinks.

Looking at this stranger, Chase speaks up saying "I guess you're a prisoner too?"

However, the old man keeps looking at the ceiling, and he tilts his head oddly from side to side. Worried, Chase then asks him in a loud voice, "Are you all right, are you hurt?"

The old man speaks in a very rough voice, like the sound a long time smoker makes. He replies, "I don't get many visitors here, not since the mine closed."

Standing up and still holding his side, Chase now asks him, "How long have you been here?"

Squinting his eyes, and puckering his lips, the old man answers, "It has been so many days and nights that I don't really know, maybe it's been years, just don't really know."

The old man now walks over to get a closer look at Chase, leaning over he says, "A young feller you are, must have gotten lost, otherwise you wouldn't be here, makes no difference." Shaking his head he fumbles around in the semi darkness.

Keeping a close eye on him, Chase is sensing that this person isn't stable, his movements seem odd, again asks him, "How long have you been a prisoner here?"

The old man looks around several times, scratches his chin, and then replies, "I reckon it's been a long time since me and my mining partner," and he now points over to a skeleton lying on the ground not far away.

"Me and ole Hank," he continues, "we were mining not far from here when these creatures jumped us and took us to this cave, and we ain't been out in the daylight sense. I think that was in 55 or was it 65, don't know, guess it don't really matter."

Realizing that the old man must have been in here a very long time not to not know if it has been days or years. Keeping his guard up, Chase now walks around, stopping very close to him and asks this feeble man, "What is your name?"

The old man puts his hand to his chin and seems to be in deep thought. Puckering his lips, and with his eyes looking up, he begins to mumble words that don't make any sense. After a minute, and clearly getting impatient, Chase firmly questions him, "Don't you even know your own name?"

The old man looks at Chase in a strange way, his eyes blinking quickly and his hands twitching, and asks, "Is the queen all right?"

Puzzled by this question, he stares at the old man for a moment, Chase isn't sure how to answer this, and motioning with his hands he says, "Your name, what is your name?"

Smiling, the old man replies, "My last name is Montgomery that I know for a fact, yes that is it. But, if that is not it, then maybe Hank knows."

Now with a blank look on his face, Chase watches as the old man glances over at the skeleton, and calls out, "Do you remember my name Hank?"

All Chase can do is shake his head; he knows that something is terribly wrong with this guy.

The old man now turns back towards Chase and answers, "Ole Hank says he doesn't remember either, but he thinks it could be Washington, or maybe Jefferson."

Chase, losing his temper and now becoming annoyed shouts, "Those are names of two Presidents you old fool."

Appearing insulted, the old man, looking over at Chase with his eyes wide open, replies, "Are you young feller, saying that I could be a president?"

Rolling his eyes and kicking the ground, Chase is now growing more impatient, as he desperately wants to find a way out of this place.

Taking a deep breath, trying to calm down, he tells the old man in a quiet voice, "I'm going to ask you one more time, what is your first name, do you know your first name?"

Now with a look of confusion on his old face, the old man now stares straight at Chase and says, "I don't know, it's been so long, that I have forgotten it." After s short pause, he goes on to say, "But it doesn't really matter."

His constant tapping of his cane on the wall is starting to irritate Chase. At this point Chase knows that this old man has spent so much time alone with these creatures and with no contact with the outside world that he must have gone insane. Feeling trapped and frustrated, Chase sits on the floor of the cave, leaning back with his head against the wall. From the cold damp floor, here he watches as the old man does the same. The old man has his head down, he begins digging with his cane, and several times he glances over at Chase. Now feeling sorry for this poor old soul, Chase begins to converse with him. After the two talk for a while, the old man does say, "I can come and go as I please, I just can't leave the cave."

Wanting to know more, Chase asks, "How did your friend die, was it an accident, or did one of those creatures kill him?"

Whipping his head around, the old man looks stunned and replies, "Ole Hank ain't dead, he just keeps to himself, ain't that right Hank," as he looks over at the skeleton.

Then turning towards Chase he says, "See, told you so, not a word, but when ole Hank does decide to start talking he won't shut up for hours, the poor feller."

Chase feels sorry for this lonely old man, to be trapped here for that long, no wonder he's nuts.

Chase asks, "How are you able to stay alive here all these years?"

The old man again stares at the ceiling, his eyes squinting and states, "The mail should be arriving today, hope I get a letter from back home."

Recognizing the signs of dementia, Chase takes a couple of deep breaths. Not wanting to get the old man agitated, but needing answers, he asks him firmly, "Do you even know what year it is?"

The old man pauses for a moment, puckers his lips and then replies, "No, but ole Hank will know." At this time the old man turns and looks at the skeleton again and calls out, "Hank, what year do you figure it is."

A few seconds pass, and the old man nods his head several times as if he is listening to someone. He now turns back towards Chase and says, "Hank says we been in these caves for four months, two weeks and five days, and I reckon he be right. Because ole Hank has always been real good with numbers, real smart he is."

With a dejected look, Chase shakes his head and replies, "You might not believe this but you've been in these caves for more than forty years."

He watches as the old man now scratches his head and puckers his mouth trying to comprehend what he has just been told to him. After a moment of silence the old man replies, "No, that ain't so, I'm gonna believe what ole Hank just told me, and you young feller are wrong."

Chase realizes that it is a waste of time trying to get a straight answer from him.

The old man then looks over at the skeleton and says, "Are you going to lay there all day, or you going to get some work done."

After a minute, the old man hits his cane on the floor and now talking in a louder voice calls out, "You're just lazy Hank, that's what you are."

He turns back towards Chase and says, "Hank won't help unless I bring him whiskey, but I ain't travelin all the way to town for a bottle of whisky." Now standing up and wiping the dirt from his pants, "No sir, I ain't going to do it, he can yell at me all he wants to."

Nervously pacing back and forth, finally throwing his arms into the air, he says, "If I buy him his whiskey he will just sit here all day drinking it, and besides when he gets drinking he gets mean. Well I remember the time a few days ago when ole Hank got so drunk that he tripped and nearly fell off the cliff that's not far from here. A long ways to the bottom it is, he could have hurt himself real bad, the poor feller."

After hearing this, Chase tells the old man, "You are crazy, you know that."

Smiling from ear to ear as his mood has changed yet again, "Crazy yes, dead no," and be lets out a small laugh, "Hee hee."

Disgusted with the old man, Chase now begins looking around for something to use as a weapon, but there is nothing here but leaves and twigs. He reluctantly asks, "What do you eat for food?"

Seeming to stare at nothing, the old man replies, "We eat real good, grass, nuts, and berries, sometimes a rabbit or a squirrel. In the spring we eat lots of fish."

Moving closer to Chase, the old man now puts his hand next to his mouth and whispers, "I don't think Hank is all there in his head," and then he winks at Chase.

Chase knows that this old crazy man won't be of any help to him in trying to escape this place, he will have to find a way out by himself, he will not end up like this old man.

The old man, hunched over and tapping his cane against the cave wall now walks over by Chase telling him in a low voice, "Follow me, young feller, there is something I want to show you."

"Old man," says Chase in a harsh tone, "you need to keep away from me. I want to get out of here, but you seem to like it here."

Again, Chase cautiously moves towards the cave entrance, carefully looking out into the tunnel, hoping that the beast has left.

The old man has now walked very near Chase and again says, "I really think that you should follow me, I promise, you won't be sorry."

Giving him a long look, and thinking over the situation with a lot of thought, Chase weighs his options. Staying here will get him nowhere, and following this insane old man gives him a bad feeling.

With a lot of hesitation and second thoughts, he decides to follow this crazy old man and see what he has to show him. Chase slowly steps out into the tunnel, remembering what happened the last time he did this, but this time there is no creature. Now following close behind the old man, who leads him out into another tunnel, then they turn down a narrow corridor.

However, it soon becomes so dark that Chase can't see where he is going and he has to put one hand on the wall and the other on the back of the old man, who seems to have no trouble finding his way in this darkness. Chase figures that the old man has been in here so long that his eyes have adapted to the dark.

The two soon stop and the old man remarks, "In this small chamber to your left is where we keep all their personal belongings."

Now hearing him say this Chase begins to get a dreadful intuition; and what did the old man mean by, "Their personal belongings."

Chase wonders if others are also being held captive here, and if so, where are they now. Chase hasn't heard any other voices, other than just his and the old mans.

Maybe this old man is just talking; after all, he does seem mentally disturbed.

He leads Chase into the chamber and tells him, "There are shoes, hats and coats here, and you can help yourself to anything in here."

Chase is still unable to see even his hand in front of his face, and tells the old man, "I can't see anything."

Which is true, it is total darkness in this part of the old mine. The old man grabs him by the hand and says, "What, are you blind," and he puts Chases hand down on what feels like clothing. Chase now feels with both hands, and the old man is right, Chase can tell that he's holding a coat, and there is a rather large pile here.

The old man says in a rather sly tone, "The owners won't mind us taking them, they don't need them anymore."

This is followed by a short hideous laugh, "They sure won't need them anymore, that's for sure."

Disturbed by these words, and still unable to see, "Just where are these owners at, are they nearby?"

He can now hear the old man start to sing, it is some old song. He knows he's heard it before but right now he doesn't remember where or when. Chase calls to him again, demanding to know where these other people are. However, the old man doesn't answer. Chase now begins to feel his way around in the dark, following the singing. To his dismay, the singing suddenly stops, and it is now so quiet that Chase gets a cold chill over his body. He is thinking that the old man has led him into a trap, where these creatures are waiting to eat him.

Clinching his fists, Chase won't go down without a fight. Pressing his back up against the wall, he stands tense and rigid. He must put his hand over his mouth, in an attempted to control his breathing, so that he can hear if something is approaching him.

After a moment of silence, and to his relief, at last the old man speaks up and says, "It looks like a full moon tonight, good for fishing."

Following the old man's jabbering, Chase finally makes his way over to him, and grabbing him tightly by the shoulders he again demands, "You better tell me right now, just where these other people are being held hostage?"

But Chase can tell by his trembling that the old man is scared, and with fear in his voice he tells Chase, "These other people were taken deep into the mountain by the hairy ones and I ain't seen them sense."

"So," Chase speaks up saying, "You mean they were killed, and you and the hairy ones ate them, isn't that true."

"No, no, no," yells the old man as he struggles to free himself, "I ain't killed anyone." He now begins to pull away, and he leads Chase out into the tunnel.

"We have to skedaddle from this part of the tunnel; else the hairy ones will think we're up to something."

Chase stays close to the old man as they wind through the tunnel and make their way back to the chamber they came from. Traveling in this total darkness has Chase very nervous, and he keeps a tight grip on the old man.

Finally, they are soon back in the chamber that they had come from. This whole time the old man is mumbling something about spirits and ghosts, and he keeps repeating, "Don't make them angry, don't make them angry"

Feeling a little safer, Chase now turns around to try to look out one of the holes, where the light is shining in through. He is hoping to see something familiar so he can get his bearings. When this proves futile, he looks behind him, only to discover that the old man is now gone. Feeling isolated, he calls to him several times, but gets no answer. After taking a moment to think what he should do next, he now starts walking over towards the chamber entrance. His plan is to turn right once out in the tunnel, and run as fast as he can towards the dim light coming in. He quickly stops dead in his tracks; his hopes of escape, thwarted when he sees a large mass block the opening.

Backing up, the reality of the situation is beginning to sink in. He is indeed a prisoner here, and he wonders what they are going to do with him. Is he to be fattened up to be eaten, or is there an even more gruesome fate awaiting him.

Believing that the old man has some kind of control over these creatures, he racks his brains trying to figure this all out.

CHAPTER 8

Sitting back down, and with a dejected look on his face Ethan feels relieved that he was able to escape the beast. However, he also realizes that sitting on this small ledge on the side of this unknown mountain could also be his final resting place.

With a rescue out of the question, he begins to think of his family. How they will never know how he died, or about the legendary creature that he saw. What of his two friends, hoping that maybe they managed to get away and are now safe. If one did by chance, make it back to the nearest town, "by the time they return and find me on this ledge I will have long since died," Ethan says with sadness. With no food or water, he knows he has maybe five days to live. That is, if he doesn't fall off this ledge while sleeping, then death will be very quick.

Night comes and Ethan has nothing to keep himself warm with, just a thin jacket. "At least I'm safe here," he says, "neither the Shadow Beasts nor any other wild animal can get at me on this ledge."

As Ethan rolls into a tight ball, his thoughts go back to Kicking Bear, and the stories he told. He remembers Kicking Bear saying that once one of these creatures comes after you it will not stop and it will never give up. He is wondering if this creature is waiting just above him, waiting for its opportunity to seek its revenge.

The long night passes, and the morning sun shines bright in Ethan's face waking him up. He knows not to stretch out; remembering that the ledge he is on is no wider than his own body. With no chance of climbing off the ledge that he's on, he now begins to think that maybe the fall to the bottom of this cliff won't kill him. He will have a slim chance of surviving, but staying here there is a zero chance.

As he leans back against the rock wall to contemplate what he knows could be a fatal decision, the wall gives in just slightly. Surprised by this, he starts to examine it closer. Ethan begins to pull several rocks away and he can now see that there is a small opening. With excitement on his face, he begins to pull more of the rocks away and his heart starts beating faster. He can see that it's a tunnel, not very big, only about two feet high and maybe three feet wide. "Maybe it is a way out," he thinks, "a way to get him off this ledge."

Looking like it could be an old mineshaft, and he's hoping, that it will lead back to one of the old mines that dot this area. He now peers into this tunnel and he knows that with it being this small that once he starts crawling into it, there will be no turning back. The tunnel is not big enough for him to turn his body around in, so there can be no second thoughts. He must continue following it, hoping and praying that it doesn't lead to a dead end.

The young man from Wisconsin now bows his head, and says a short prayer. He next makes the sign of the cross on his chest, looks up, grits his teeth, and he begins crawling forward into the darkness. Crawling through this narrow space, Ethan must control his urge to panic; the fear of being in confined spaces has always been a curse for him since he was young. This condition has plagued him his whole life, and as he was growing up, he was unable to go into closets or storage sheds, and taking an elevator was out of the question. At one point his condition became so bad for him that just getting into a car caused him to break out into a cold sweat. Medication had controlled most of his fears and as he got older, he learned to hide this condition from others. Only rarely now did this affliction show itself, but when it did he always had others around him. With their encouragement and support, he made it through these episodes of panic and was able to lead a normal life.

However, here in this dark and narrow tunnel, he is alone. There will be no help, no one to tell him that everything is going to be all right. He has stopped several times, when he begins to hyperventilate. He tells himself repeatedly, "Stay calm, stay focused." When he feels he is in control again, he takes a deep breath and begins moving forward.

Starting to get worried as the hours pass and still no end to this tunnel. He begins to have doubts, "Maybe," he contemplates, "it is a dead end, and I will soon be trapped with no way to turn around, maybe this will be my tomb."

Each time these negative thoughts enter his head he remembers his father always telling him, "No matter how bad a situation looks, how dire and hopeless it seems, don't ever quit, and never lose your faith."

With his Fathers words on his lips, Ethan begins crawling forward again. The air is now beginning to get thin and it causes him to stop and rest more often than he wants to. He carries a lighter in his pocket, but using it will use up precious oxygen. After each stop, it becomes more and more difficult to get moving again, and it takes more effort to stay mentally focused. He is by now breathing in deep breaths; Ethan knows he is running out of oxygen. After his last stop he had to lay his head down, with the thin air he is having trouble staying awake. His body just wants to quit, it is telling him that it can go no further. However, a voice in his head tells him, "Get up, and keep moving!"

Determined not to die in this dark and forbidding place, Ethan once again raises himself up and on shaking knees and with arms that feel numb he tells himself "I will not quit."

Once more, he begins moving forward, with darkness all around him it is impossible for him to tell just how far he has traveled. He estimates he has gone several miles, maybe as many as ten. However, this is only a guess. When exhaustion, dehydration, and fatigue finally are too much, he collapses to the ground. At the start of his journey, he had been moving quickly through the tunnel and covered a lot of ground. But as time went by his progress has slowed, and now Ethan crawls along inch by inch. He has made himself a promise, to use every ounce of energy he has left in his body, and when his arms and legs no longer respond, he will then stop, but only then.

As he summons up yet another round of strength to continue, and builds up his confidence for one more effort, all hope suddenly leaves him when his head hits a dirt wall. Putting his hands out in front of him, Ethan can feel that the tunnel goes no farther; it has come to a dead end. Quickly touching all around, and with a sense of desperation, he realizes that the tunnel has indeed stopped here. His worst nightmare has come true. If it did lead to one of the old mining shafts, this part of the tunnel must have collapsed. He knows, after all, that it has been years since they were last used.

Dejected, and heartbroken, he now lays on his back, and he calls aloud, "This is it, this is where I will die."

He knows that no one will ever find his body; it will stay here in this nameless grave forever. A smile now crosses his face when he thinks of his family. How his parents had put off their dream vacation so that they could use that money to send him to college. The memories begin flashing through his mind, at least he will die with a smile on his face, and several tears now roll down his cheeks.

Closing his eyes, he asks God, "Take care of my parents during their grieving; they are good people. As for my brother and sister, please watch over them, they are young and inexperienced in life, steer them the right way. Don't let them do foolish things, like camping in the middle of nowhere." He begins to laugh at his last statement.

As Ethan now waits for the end, and while staring up into the darkness, something catches his attention. He blinks his eyes; as he can see a very small light just above his head. He wonders if it is an angel coming for him. When the light doesn't get any closer, reaching up he realizes that he can touch where the light is coming from. As his excitement grows, he begins wiping his hand back and forth on this light, and now the light grows bigger. Fresh air now fills his lungs, "This," he says with enthusiasm, "is a miracle."

He now pushes up with both hands, and the surface moves, just slightly but it did move. He knows instantly that this is a door, a possible way out. But where did it lead, he didn't know and it didn't matter as long as he gets out of this dark and gloomy tunnel.

Hoping and praying that this is not some cruel hallucination, and giving him a false sense of liberation. Concentrating all his strength, again, he pushes up and the door moves a little more this time. With dirt falling down on his face, he must stops to wipe his eyes.

CHAPTER 9

Joseph has sat in this small isolated shack all night, expecting that at any moment the Shadow Beasts will come crashing through the door and kill him. However, the night remained quiet, and he is very surprised and bewildered by this.

At this moment, Joseph is contemplating what to do, should he take a chance and leave the safety of the shack. Knowing full well that these creatures will be waiting just inside the forest, where they will easily catch him, or should he remain right here where he's safe.

He now sits back against the wall tapping his finger on his forehead, with his friends gone; he knows he will be next. The hours pass, and still not one Shadow Beast has attacked the old shack. He is wondering and trying to come up with a logical explanation on what these creatures are waiting on. Looking at the holes in the ceiling, and how the walls are ready to fall apart, he knows that this old shack is not a safe place. Joseph grabs the handle of an old pickaxe and decides to leave the shack, if he is to die, he'll die fighting. He will do the brave thing, even if it costs him his life; it is what his ancestors would do.

With a look of confidence on his face, Joseph now stands up and turns towards the door. He pauses for a moment to recite an old Indian creed, (Do not fear going forward, fear only standing still.) He is hoping that these words will give him the courage and motivation that he needs.

With his hand on the door latch, he is just about to open the door when a noise from behind catches his attention. Turning around quickly, and tensing up, he scans the small room. With his heart racing, he grips the handle of the pickaxe so tightly that his knuckles are turning white.

Believing that it must finally be the Shadow Beasts coming for him, and they have somehow gotten inside the old shack. The sweat starts to roll down his face as he recalls that his grandfather did say that these Shadow Beasts could make themselves invisible. Part of him still can't believe that these creature really exist, and that they have these special powers. However, deep in his soul another part is beginning to awaken long suppressed feelings and yearnings.

After not seeing or hearing any more sounds or movements, Joseph tries desperately to decide if he should turn and run out of there, or face this unknown.

Before he can decide, he is startled when he sees a small section of the floor start to move. His first thought is that these Shadow Beasts have dug under the shack and are coming up through the floorboards. With the pickaxe now tight in his grip, he holds it up high over his head, and steps towards the movement on the floor. He can hear something, an almost like a human voice, "But it can't be," he mumbles.

He knows these creatures are very tricky, and that they are trying to fool him. Standing at the ready, a very nervous and fearful Joseph is determined to strike the first blow. Suddenly the door on the floor flies open and Joseph screams, he is about to bury the pickaxe into the skull of one of these creatures.

To his surprise and relief, he sees Ethan gasping for air as he tries to climb up and out of the hole. Joseph immediately throws the axe down and grabs his friend, pulling him up and out of the hole. Next, he gently lays him on the floor, shaking his head in disbelief. Ethan, who is now starting to cry, looks at Joseph and says, "It is so good to see you old friend."

Joseph is now sitting on the floor holding Ethan on his lap, telling him, "Everything is going to be all right."

After several minutes, Ethan is able to sit up and he begins to tell Joseph about going over the cliff and then how he began crawling through the tunnel. After coughing several times, Ethan says, "It is a miracle that I'm still alive."

"I thought that the creature had gotten you, that when I got to this shack, I looked back but I saw no movement in the tall grass."

Struggling to hold his head up, "The Shadow Beast chased me from the field to the edge of a cliff," replies Ethan as he rubs his hand across his face.

Needing a moment to calm down, Ethan continues, "At least we are both safe at the moment, but we must get back to the camp and find Chase so that we can all leave this place."

Helping his friend sit up, Joseph tells him, "I was about to leave, another five minutes and I would have been gone."

The two young men now talk about a plan of escape, and they hope that nothing has happened to Chase. With just one pickaxe as their only weapon, it will be difficult if not impossible for them to fight the Shadow Beasts.

"I did find a rifle in here but it has no bullets," a dejected Joseph says.

The two sit in silence, one completely exhausted, but grateful to be out of that tunnel. The other hoping he is enough like his Grandfather to get him and his friends out of this mess.

Being young and stubborn, the two have a strong conviction that they can figure a way out of this situation.

After resting and regaining his strength, Ethan starts to search the shack for anything that might be of use. In the far corner, he makes a remarkable discovery; in several old crates, he finds some dynamite. Holding one up and with eyes wide open and grinning from ear to ear, "This," he declares, "could be the miracle we have been looking for."

Digging in his pocket, he is relieved to find that his lighter is there and that it's not broken. Neither he nor Joseph has ever handled dynamite before, so they are very careful removing them from the crates. Ethan puts five sticks of dynamite in his belt while Joseph says, "I'll just carry mine in my hands."

Now the two have what they think will be enough to stop these Shadow Beasts. Joseph speaks up telling Ethan, "Just make sure when you light the fuse, that you through the dynamite far away from us."

With a sneer, Ethan replies, "When I was in high school, I was able to through a baseball from the outfield all the way to home plate. So I think I can manage to do that, and don't worry," he continues, acting in a brash way, "I know what I'm doing."

As Joseph rolls his eyes at his over confident friend, Ethan takes a few steps and then slips and falls. This causes several sticks of dynamite to fall from his belt and land on the ground between the two.

Instinctively they drop to the dirt floor, and with their hearts racing, both young men coward down. They are expecting that at any time the explosion is going to blow them to pieces. However, after a moment and to their surprise nothing happens. Slowly removing their hands from their faces, gradually getting to their feet, and looking at each other, a small laugh breaks out between them. They realize that the dynamite won't explode until the fuse is lit.

After waiting until their heartbeats have slowed down, Joseph remarks, "Let's try to make it out of this shack without killing ourselves, okay."

Flashing a devious grin, a slightly embarrassed Ethan replies, "It won't happen again, I'll be more careful."

Taking one more look out the small window, the two feel confident that there are no shadow beats in the area.

They now set out for their camp, hoping to leave this area and its strange occupants. Joseph still has the pickaxe, neither one knowing for sure, if the dynamite that they carry will even work. They realize that after all, that the dynamite has been sitting in that old shack for who knows how many years.

Ethan suggests, "Why don't I light one of the dynamite sticks to know for sure that it does actually work."

However, Joseph tells him, "The loud noise will attract the Shadow Beasts to our location, we can not light them."

Ethan understands and he nodes his head in agreement. "You're right; we should try and be as quiet as possible."

Therefore, for now, they must assume that the dynamite still works. Both young men praying that a situation never comes up, to where they must use them.

They must now travel light and fast, but with Ethan suffering from dehydration, he is weak and unable to maintain a fast pass. After they have stopped several times for Ethan to rest, Joseph knows what he has to do. Therefore, when they stop again he helps Ethan laid down on the ground. Joseph now finds several small trees about three inches in diameter, breaking them into six-foot lengths and removing their branches. He next lays them on the ground and he now removes his jacket and shirt, sliding them over the two trees. He has made a sturdy gurney to carry his friend on.

Patting Joseph on the back, Ethan is impressed, "You're survival knowledge is very good," he says with a smile.

As he lays down on the makeshift gurney, Ethan closes his eyes, fighting the urge to fall asleep. With his body aching and suffering from dehydration, he begins to drift in and out of consciousness. After making sure that his friend is securely strapped in, Joseph grabs the ends of the gurney and picking them up he begins dragging it down the path. They cover a lot more ground this way, and Ethan is able to rest and conserve his strength.

On they move, not looking back, as Joseph knows that he must keep a steady pace if he is to have any chance of escaping the Shadow Beasts. Once in awhile Joseph calls back to ask Ethan how he is doing, Ethan would reply, "I'm doing fine, thank you for helping me, and I owe you big time for this."

Joseph knows that time isn't on their side, so he decides to take a shorter route back to their camp. This new route will bring them close to some of the old mines, which he has a strong feeling is maybe where these Shadow Beasts might be living. It is a chance he is willing to take; this shorter route will save miles and valuable time.

Without telling Ethan his decision, Joseph now goes in the direction of the old mines. The ground is much smoother here, the land is flat and it is barren of trees, the aftermath of the mining industry, and Joseph can maintain a good pace. Mile after mile he pulls his friend, when he begins to get tired, Joseph starts to have doubts that they will ever make it back. He pulls out from his pocket, a bear's claw that was given to him by the medicine man in his tribe. He was told that this bear claw is said to possess powers that will call on his ancestors when he is in danger. Joseph never much believed in the supernatural like the rest of his tribe. He has gone the way of the white man as others in his tribe would say about him. He thought the stories about spirits, and one being able to see visions, was just made up, and that it was foolish talk by the old people in his tribe. With encouragement and prodding from his Grandfather, Joseph always carried the bear claw with him.

However, as Joseph sits here on the ground resting, he suddenly can see an eagle fly overhead. He watches it majestically circles him several times, and for a brief moment, he is mesmerized by its graceful flight. Lowering his head and needing just another minute of rest before he starts pulling the gurney again. Hoping that the worst is behind him and Ethan, and soon they will be out of these woods.

Always keeping a watchful eye, he takes a glance over to the nearby forest. Jumping back, he is shocked to see a wolf and a bear standing side by side watching him. He quickly gets to his feet without taking his eyes off the two animals. Curious and wondering at why would these two natural enemies, be so close to each other, and the two not be fighting. He watches with confusion, as the bear and the wolf now begin a slow deliberate walk towards him. Doing his best not to panic, he picks up his pickaxe. He moves next to Ethan while trying to find a good spot to defend himself.

As the seconds go by, he becomes more frightened, constantly looking around in the hopes of finding a way out of this bizarre situation.

However, within minutes the two animals are now only a short distance from him when they stop, and he notices that their eyes are a glowing red. He now starts to recall the stories that his grandfather had told him about how the bear and the wolf had come to his aid when he was dying in the forest. They had eyes of red he would say, and they dragged him by his clothing back to his tribe. His grandfather was sure that the Great Spirit had sent them.

Joseph had no other explanation for the behavior of these two wild animals. He gazes with astonishment, as these two strange acting animals now stand motionless in front of him. Despite his attempts at trying to scare these creatures away, they remained perfectly still. They don't attack him nor do they run away. Again, trying his best not to panic, Joseph now begins to get an odd feeling. With the air around him suddenly getting cold, he feels a presents that he has never felt before. Taking a deep breath and getting on his knees, he calls on the spirits of his ancestors to give him the strength he needs. Joseph has by now, begun to understand some of the wisdom that his grandfather had tried for so many years to teach him. He can remember him saying, "Let the Great Spirit guide you when you have become lost, to call on the Ghosts of the Ancient ones for strength."

Joseph wishes his grandfather were here with him right now. Looking back up into the sky, he now sees great white clouds against a blue backdrop. Just moments before, there were no clouds, and it had been very hot and muggy. Closing his eyes he reaches into his soul, calling on forces he thought didn't exist.

A loud high pitch sound now pierces the forest, quickly opening his eyes; Joseph can see a magnificent eagle soaring across the sky. This one animal is the most sacred of his people, it signifies bravery, wisdom, and it is a good omen. Joseph knows at that moment that he was wrong to have turned away from his grandfathers teachings. As the eagle flies closer, Joseph suddenly feels a force enter his body. His senses are more alert; he sniffs the air, he listens to the sounds around him. With eyes focused, he begins to scan the area ahead of him. He repeats to himself, "Be brave, be strong, and believe in what you have been told."

With that said Young Joseph Browndeer quickly gets to his feet, with chin up and his chest sticking out, he feels rejuvenated. Reaching down he once again grabs the gurney and begins to pull it faster than before, his foot strikes are silent and swift. The pride is showing on his face, after all he is the grandson of Kicking Bear.

Joseph is now following directly behind the bear and the wolf as they lead the way. The more he watches these two animals, the more confident and self assured he becomes. Entranced by their graceful movements and actions, he feels as if a great weight has been lifted from his shoulders. After a short time, Joseph is startled when before his very eyes he watches the bear and the wolf vanish into a mist. Still stunned by what he has just witnessed, he now can see a figure coming in from his left; it is a ghostly apparition riding a pure white horse.

Backing up a few steps, Joseph recognizes it, the elders have told of this phantom rider. They called it the Ghost Warrior, and that it will appear in times of danger. Looking closer Joseph sees that it is a member of his tribe; only this person had died many years ago.

The Ghost Warrior stops ten yards from Joseph, with its hair waving as if being blown by the wind, and the pure white horse suddenly rearing up on its hind legs. Joseph finds himself now locked in the gaze of this ghost. The Ghost Warrior now points his spear to the area ahead and looking in that direction Joseph can see a vision. In this vision, it is he and his two friends, Ethan and Chase, and they are hugging each other. He notices that Ethan is on crutches and his right leg is in a cast. He also sees that his own right shoulder is heavily taped up, and a bandage is across his forehead. Now he watches them get into a car and drive away.

Joseph knows that this vision tells him that they will all make it out of here alive, and when he turns back, the Ghost Warrior is gone.

At this time, Joseph snaps out of his trance when he hears Ethan begin to sit up and say, "I feel much better now."

Looking at Joseph, who is staring out across the barren landscape as if he is in a trance, Ethan asks his friend, "Are you alright?"

Slowly turning his head he replies, "I'm fine, and I know that everything is going to be all right."

Running his fingers through his hair and trying to focus his eyes, Ethan asks, "Why are you so sure all of a sudden, when before you doubted we would even make it out of here alive?"

Joseph, who now clutches the bear claw in his hand, answers firmly, "My ancestors gave me a vision."

Nodding his head, "Very well," replies Ethan, "if you say so."

Ethan is now able to stand, and as he looks around, he comments, "I don't recognize any of this, where are we?"

Joseph speaks up saying, "I have chosen to take this way because it will be a shorter route back to our camp."

"Have you seen anything unusual while I was sleeping," asks Ethan.

With a smile and a wink, "I have seen a great many things, but nothing unusual."

The two now walk across the barren landscape, and they can see the caves at the base of a mountain.

Joseph tells Ethan, "These are the old mining caves, and we should avoid them, who knows," he says with hesitation, "at what might be living in them."

Taking his word on this, Ethan must rely on his friend to get them both out of this area and back to their camp.

As the two are making a wide arch away from the caves, Ethan notices something sparkle on the ground in the distance. He immediately goes to investigate, Joseph stays where he is, constantly looking around for any movement in the nearby woods. Upon reaching this sparkly object, Ethan reaches down and picking it up, and after just a few seconds he calls back to Joseph telling him, "You better come up here and take a look at this."

Joseph now hurries and when he sees what Ethan is holding in his hand his heart sinks, what Ethan has found is Chases watch. Both know that this means that the Shadow Beasts have taken Chase from their camp and that they have brought him here to these old mines.

Puzzled, Ethan asks, "So why didn't the Shadow Beasts kill him back at the camp, why bring him here?"

Joseph replies, "Maybe they did kill him, and they just brought his body back here."

Joseph isn't sure just why the Shadow Beasts had brought Chase here, the longer he thinks about it the more he begins to get a sick feeling in his stomach about it.

Now showing some fear on his face and in his voice, Ethan asks, "Do these Shadow Beasts eat people?"

After a moment, Joseph replies, "I have never heard that any of these Shadow Beasts have ever eaten anyone. However, if they do eat people," he utters, "no one has lived to tell about it."

Seeing that Ethan is able to walk, they won't need the gurney any longer, Joseph now puts his shirt and jacket back on.

Now as the two walk closer to the caves, the ground now turns from gravel to sand and they can clearly see huge footprints all around. Joseph was not expecting this; he had been hoping to avoid a confrontation with these Shadow Beasts.

Both young men now stand staring at the caves, and then they look at each other.

Taking a deep breath and swallowing hard, Ethan speaks up saying, "You know we have to go in there and find Chase."

Gritting his teeth, Joseph replies, "You know that Chase may not even be alive; the Shadow Beasts may have already killed him."

Shaking his head defiantly, "Doesn't matter," answers Ethan sternly, "I'm going in there with or without you, and I'm bringing him out with me whether he's alive or dead."

Joseph puts his hand on Ethan's shoulder and says, "It is a foolish thing that you are going to do, but it is also very brave. I can not let you go alone; we will go together my brother."

Now the two begin a slow walk towards the old mines, and each is thinking that once inside they may never see daylight again.

CHAPTER 10

Chase now backs up against the far wall; he knows he can't fight this beast without a weapon. Still, it's not in his nature to give up, and he decides that if he can take a rock and hit this creature hard enough in the head that it may give him a chance of escaping. He also knows the dangers, by taking this risk, that he may only anger this beast, and that it will then turn its rage on him. Taking a couple of deep breaths, Chase paces the small chamber, constantly looking at the entrance only to see the creature also pacing just outside. He knows that his plan won't work, there is just no way that he can sneak up behind the creature without it seeing him first. Still, Chase decides that he would rather die fighting than slowly die here. He has decided that he won't eat any food brought in by the old man, still thinking that he is being fattened up so they can eat him.

After several minutes Chase manages to loosen a rock from the cave wall, it's the size of a bowling ball. Knowing that he'll only get one shot at this, he begins walking towards the creature, but suddenly the old man walks in and tells Chase, "You need to come with me young feller."

Hesitant and skeptical of the whole situation, Chase demands to know from this old man, "Just where are you taking me?"

Waving his hands, the old man replies, "It is something that may interest you."

"Also," the old man adds, as he points, "That rock you have in your hands won't put a scratch on this animal's head, so you might as well put it down."

With much hesitation, Chase drops the rock and reluctantly begins to follow the old man out of the chamber. He is lead for a few minutes down the dark tunnel, when he begins to see a slight glow shinning out into the tunnel from one of the chambers just ahead. Chase, getting more nervous by the minute, is very puzzled by this, but he keeps walking. As he tilts his head to look into this chamber, he can see that the interior of the room is very well lit. The light is coming from numerous glowing rocks arranged in a circle on the floor; each of these rocks is the size of a softball. In the center of these lights, Chase can see lying on a stone table is one of these creatures, but it is much smaller than the others that he has seen.

The old man now tells Chase, "You need to move closer to it, don't be afraid," he says as he motions with his hand.

As the two begin to get near this creature, Chase is startled to see several of these beasts standing a short distance away. His first reaction is to grab the old man, thinking that this is a trap. Holding the old man in a bear hug, Chase tells him, "You better order these creatures to stay back, or else."

The old man tells him, "Calm down young man, they will not harm you."

Chase calls in an angry voice, "You set me up; you brought me here so that those creatures can eat me."

Gasping for air, as Chase's grip around his neck has tightened. The old man now says, "You have it all wrong, if you let me go I'll explain everything to you."

Chase realizes that the creatures haven't moved, they have made no attempt to come towards him. After thinking about this for a few seconds, he decides not to let the old man go, he tells him instead, "Start explaining."

The old man now tells Chase, "The creature lying on the table in front of you has a gunshot wound, and it is dying. However," he says, "I know nothing about doctoring."

After a short pause, he asks Chase, "Will you please look at this injured creature, and see what you can do to help it."

Looking over at this creature, Chase can indeed see that it has been injured, as there is lots of blood on its fur and on the table. He releases the old man and steps towards the creature, turning he asks, "What happened to this creature, how did it get injured?"

Rubbing his neck, the old man replies, "This is the one that you shot."

Chase, somewhat surprised answers back, "How do you know it was me?"

The old man looks at Chase and says, "These creatures know everything that happens in these woods, and they told me that you shot it."

Chase is silent for a moment, this is beginning to get really weird; and he has thoughts of turning and running as fast as he can.

The old man speaks up saying, "Normally these creatures are very timid and shy, but not when someone hurts one of them. It is the only time that I have ever seen them angry." Walking closer, he now asks Chase, "Is there anything possible that you can do to help this creature?"

Chase does have training in first aid, and he is training to become a doctor, but he has just started his studies at the university. He really doesn't know the first thing about operating on someone, let alone a creature like this.

Shrugging his shoulders, he says, "I have watched a few procedures, but that's it."

The old man looks intensely at Chase and declares, "I think you better come up with a plan to save this creature, if not," he now looks down at the floor, "it's been nice knowing you."

Chase didn't think that it was possible to get any more nervous and scared than he already is. However, after hearing the old man say that, now he is scared, more so than ever in his life.

Chase swallows hard, and then taking a quick glance at the creatures standing not far away, he now steps closer to this small creature lying on the table. It is moving slightly back and forth, he can hear it moan, it is obviously in pain. He can see that the bullet entered in its lower right side, so he reaches over grabbing it, as he needs to try to turn it over to check for an exit wound.

Upon seeing this, the other creatures standing nearby begin grunting and throwing their arms into the air. Chase immediately stops, fearing they are going to hurt him. To his surprise, he sees the old man step in and with a few hand signs, the creatures quickly calm down. Once more, Chase finds himself stunned and amazed by this old man's actions. How he has such control over these wild animals, it is very intriguing to Chase. The old man now turns towards Chase and says, "It is okay to proceed now, they won't bother you."

He notices that the old man is suddenly talking very clear and in complete sentences, this has him confused.

After staring at the old man for a few seconds, Chase turns back to the small creature lying in front of him. He now continues to roll it onto its side, glancing up to see the reaction of the other creatures, he is surprised and relieved when none of them move. He is glad to see an exit wound, this means that the bullet has gone completely through its body. Chase just needs to sew up the wounds. However, he has no sutures, not even a needle and thread. Telling the old man this, Chase is surprised when the old man tells him, "You just stay put and I will be right back."

The old man now hurries out of the room, his feet no longer shuffling across the floor. While waiting for his return, Chase looks into the faces of these creatures, they seem sad and concerned now. Nevertheless, they are just animals, he thinks, they are not supposed to show feelings.

To him, they are no longer these terrifying man-eaters. They have a look on their faces that is almost human like. They remain very quiet, and move about very little, which gives Chase the impression that they actually know that what he is doing is important.

The female has her head down, and Chase isn't sure if she is crying or simply making their usual noises. The big male on the right lifts its arm out towards Chase. Not knowing what to do now, Chase is about to do the same when the old man comes rushing back into the room quickly and hands Chase a small black leather bag.

"Here" he says slightly out of breath, "This should contain everything, all the medical supplies you will need to stop the hemorrhaging. There are sutures in here and even a syringe containing a mild sedative."

Upon hearing this, Chase's first thought is, "How does an old miner that has been living in these caves for all these years come up with words like that." Another question, "Where did he get this medical bag," or does Chase even want to know. These questions and others will have to wait; first Chase needs to fix up his first patient. While he is closing up the wounds on the small creature, he notices that the old man no longer walks with the aid of a cane. The old man occasionally would make a hand sign towards the creatures, which, to Chases surprise would then make a sign back to him.

"This is incredible;" Chase says to himself, "This old man is actually communicating with these wilds beasts."

Chase continues sewing up his patient, and he thinks that if he ever makes it out of here, how funny it will be to tell people that his very first patient was a hairy monster.

Finally, he is done, and as he backs up the old man comes over to him, putting his hand on Chase's shoulder, he says, "Looks like you did a fine job, you will make an excellent doctor." Chase, now taking a step back and wide eyed, is yet again, shocked by this old man's words. First how did this old man know that he is studying to become a doctor, second, he wants to know who the hell is this old man. Chase stands back, giving him a long look, trying to understand this whole situation.

The old man motions for Chase to follow him, but Chase says, "No, not till you tell me who you really are and what is going on around here."

Nodding his head, "Very well" he replies, "If you insist, I think you better sit down."

Apprehensive and uneasy at what this old man is about tell him, Chase keeps one eye on the old man and one eye on the door. The two now walk over to several crude looking wooden chairs sitting against the wall. Getting himself comfortable, the old man now speaks up and says, "I made these two chairs myself, not bad for a Harvard grad."

Sitting back in his chair and rolling his eyes, "You're no Harvard Grad," an angry Chase replies.

With a smile and a wink, "Don't be so sure of yourself young man."

"I'm sure of one thing and that is you are nuts."

Believing now that the old man is insane, Chase stands up and heads for the door.

"Just give me one minute of your time, that's all I ask."

Stopping, Chase debates if he should give him his one minute, or should he just leave.

Chase watches in amazement, as the old man begins to remove his long white beard, and he lays it on his lap. He now looks up at Chase, whose eyes are wide open. The old man continues to remove the rest of his disguise. Chase stutters as he speaks up saying, "Your beard is a fake; the way you walk and talk is a fake. Why on earth, would you dress and act like a senile old man?"

With a slight grin, the old man now looks straight at Chase and replies, "Let me introduce myself, I'm Professor Andrew Montgomery, and I'm from the San Francisco Zoo, I work in the primate department there. I have been studying these remarkable creatures for nearly ten years."

By the expression now on Chase's face, this news is shocking to him.

Needing to sit down, "Why," he asks, now leaning forward, "Would you go through all this trouble of pretending to be a crazy old man?"

"Because," the Professor answers, "the existence of these unknown creatures has to remain a secret. If the outside world were to find out that these animals are real, this place will be over run with photographers, animals rights activists and even hunters wanting to claim one as a trophy. I needed time to study them, to learn everything I can about them. They are quite intelligent, as you have witnessed yourself. I'm able to communicate with them using sign language."

Taking a big breath, Chase begins to shake his head; "This" he states, "is just unbelievable." Now forcing a smile, "Your acting is very good," Chase tells him, "It had me completely fooled." The two laugh for a moment, and then getting serious again, "What about that skeleton I saw, and the pile of clothes?"

The Professor smiles, "The skeleton is a fake, I bought it at a goodwill store and as for the clothing, they are mine."

Chase has to stand up after hearing this, and he starts rubbing his chin.

He is still amazed at the disguise and acting job that Professor Montgomery pulled on him.

Looking around Chase asks, "And these glowing rocks, what are they?"

The Professor answers, "They are just battery powered lights, with a plastic covering. You see these creatures didn't like the bright light given off by my lantern, so I had a friend of mine make these up for me."

Taking a glance over at the Shadow Beasts, he notices that they have remained very calm this whole time.

"How did you learn that these creatures even lived here," Chase inquires, as he has gotten over his initial shock.

Now sitting back in his chair, the Professor answers, "Some of my colleagues and I had heard rumors for years that a large hairy beast that walks on two legs lived in this area. Yes, they were just rumors, and no one had any physical proof that these creatures really existed. However, I knew that as foolish as they sounded, that it was possible for just such an animal to exist in these deep and remote forests. The Native Americans have told stories about these creatures that go back hundreds of years. So I knew that there was some truth in these rumors."

The Professor now sits on the edge of his chair, and tells Chase, "These creatures are in my opinion the remnants of an extinct ape called Gigantopithecus. They are a genus of ape that existed roughly one million years to as recently as three hundred thousand years ago. These apes," he continues, "lived in China at that time, and must have crossed the land bridge that was at that time the Bering Straits, and migrated south to this region."

Chase finds the Professors theory fascinating, "Please continue, I want to learn more about these creatures."

The Professor is anxious to inform his young friend, happy to be able to finally share in his remarkable discovery with someone,

"I came here ten years ago," he begins, "when a friend of mine told me that he had spotted what looked like a gorilla in an open field while flying his plane low over this area. After hearing this, I had to go myself and to see if I could make contact with these creatures. I decided to search by myself, but after two weeks, I came up empty. However, on my way back I stopped at an Indian Reservation, looking for more clues and maybe finding someone that had actually seen one of these creatures. After asking around, I was soon taken to meet the Tribal Elder who they said could answer my questions. I was escorted a short distance through the woods until we came out and into a clearing. With logs forming a great circle, it looked like it was a place where they must hold their Pow wow's. On the opposite side, I could see an elder gentleman sitting on the ground in front of a totem pole with his legs crossed.

A small fire burned a short distance away, and it all seemed very peaceful. My escort had by now left, so I walked abruptly around the circle of logs and sat on the ground in front of him. As I sat across from him, he opened his eyes and we looked at each other for a moment in silence.

Then this Tribal Elder spoke in a quiet voice, he startled me by asking why I have come seeking the hairy ones that live deep in the forest.

I was taken aback that he knew this about me, so I replied that if these creature truly do exist, then they need to be protected and studied.

At that moment, I introduced myself to him, letting him know that I was not going to hurt these creatures, or even try to capture one. I just wanted to study and understand their behavior, as that is my job. The elder said that yes, the time has come, that the white man should know about these Shadow Beasts. However, he added, that I was the only one that can know where these creatures live, and that he will only take me there, no one else. This is how I began studying these animals."

Getting a strange feeling that he knows just who this elder is, Chase asks, "Can you tell me the name of the Tribal Elder?"

"I don't see the harm in revealing his name; after all you have already seen these creatures yourself."

Now taking a moment to wipe some dirt from his face, the Professor answers, "The elders name is Kicking Bear."

Chase now drops his mouth open, and replies, "I know Kicking Bear, my friends and I just met him a few days ago."

Smiling at hearing this, "I hope he is doing well," answers the professor, "I don't get to see and talk with him as often as I would like to."

Feeling that he can trust and confide in Chase, he now asks, "I have named each of these animals, would you care to know their names?"

With confusion still on his face, Chase throws his hands into the air and replies, "Sure why not."

The two stand up and the professor now points at the three large animals standing not far away, and begins, "The one on the right I call Puyallup, which means Shadow. The one in the middle, which I'm sure you have noticed is a female, I call her Hurit, which means Beautiful. Then the one on the left is call Kajika, which means Walks without sound. The smaller one laying on the table his name is Alsoomse, which means Independent."

Chase smiles politely, "Those are good names, but how did you come up with them, they sound Indian."

Professor Montgomery replies, "To be truthful, I didn't come up with those names, it was Kicking Bear."

"So," answers Chase "Then Kicking Bear has visited you here."

"Yes," the Professor replies, "and without his help and guidance I don't think it would have been possible for me to do this research. As far as I know, he is the only other person that knows that these creatures are living in these mines."

Doing his best to absorb and comprehend all this information, looking around he asks, "Are these four creatures all that there is or are there any more?"

With his face turning gloomy, the Professor replies, "No, there is one more, and that one has refused to communicate with me. The Native tribes call this one animal, Atahsaia, which means, The Cannibal Demon. It has resisted all my attempts and efforts to get close to him. Several times, it has even attacked me, and if it weren't for these others that came to my aid and protected me, I would have been killed."

A little apprehensive after hearing this, Chase asks, "Where is this Cannibal Demon at right now?"

The Professor answers, "It lives in the forest, and on occasion, it will visit these old mining caves. It is very bad tempered, and I'm sure if anyone was to accidently run into it, unlike the others who would avoid any contact with people, this one would probably do something very violent to them."

Chase, still scratching his head at what has happened in the last ten minutes, says, "I have just one more question." Walking around trying to sort out this incredible occurrence, this once in a lifetime experience, he now asks the Professor, "Just how are you able tell one of these animals from another?"

With his finger in the air, the Professor begins by saying; "You see the one that has a gray streak of fur on its shoulder, that one is called, Kajika."

Before the professor could answer any further, they hear someone calling from out in the tunnel. "Are you in there Joseph?"

Chase immediately recognizes the voice and jumping to his feet, shouts, "That it is my friend Ethan."

At that very instant; the ground begins to shake, and Chase puts his hands against the wall to steady himself. Debris and rubble begins falling from the ceiling, and dust fills the air. This tremor has lasted longer than just a few seconds, and the ground beneath their feet vibrates. The Professor and Chase both now must move quickly against the wall to avoid being injured by falling debris. When the shaking stops, they can see that the tunnel just to the left of the chamber, where they had heard Ethan calling from, has collapsed. After several minutes, the two stand up, shaken up but unhurt, Chase hurries out into the tunnel. Looking through the dust, he is distraught when he sees that a wall of dirt and rock has sealed it up completely.

Chase now franticly yells, "We have to dig out my friend!"

However, the Professor quickly puts his hand on Chases shoulder, holding him back, replies, "Your friend is already dead."

"He can't be, you're wrong, he's alive I know it."

Trying to console the grief stricken young man, "I'm sorry, but no one could survive that many tons of rock and dirt falling on them."

Chase now puts his head down, "Ethan was so close, if he had been just a little closer he would be safe right now."

"There is nothing you could have done to prevent this tragedy, it is a terrible accident."

"I can't believe he's dead," pausing for a moment to get control of his emotions. Looking over at the professor with glassy eyes and needing to take a deep breath, "He was my friend."

With a warm smile, "I'm sure he considered you a friend also."

The Professor now replies, "These tremors are occurring more frequently, and I'm trying to find another location for these animals before this whole mountain comes crashing down."

Looking back into the room, Chase can see that the tremors have caused these animals to go into an almost panic state. The Professor quickly goes over to them and in a short while, he is able to calm them down. He now walks back over to Chase telling him, "These tremors had started about a year ago and they have been getting worse ever since, and it is important that I find a safe place for these animals very soon."

Chase doesn't want to leave, but realizing that there is nothing he can do for his friend, and with a heavy heart he tells the Professor, "I will help you get these creatures out of here and into a safer place."

Nodding his head in appreciation, and patting the young man on the shoulder the Professor now walks back over to the creatures and makes a few hands signs. Chase watches as these creatures go over to the table, and the big one called Kajika, gently picks up the injured one. The Shadow Beasts now walk single file out into the tunnel; he and the Professor follow close behind.

CHAPTER 11

Ethan and Joseph both take a deep breath and with a stick of dynamite in each hand, they begin a slow walk towards the cave entrance. Just then, the ground begins to shake.

This causes both young men to have a look of fear on their faces. This is not what they needed, as things were already dangerous enough. When the ground stops shaking, a nervous Ethan comments, "This whole area must be unstable. The miners must have over mined here and this whole area has so many tunnels and caves that it could collapse at any time."

Hearing this, Joseph knows that a dangerous situation has just become even worse. Now besides dealing with these beasts they will also have to worry about the possibility of being buried alive from a cave in.

Regaining their composure, the two walk forward very cautiously, constantly looking around making sure these beasts don't get behind them.

With no flashlights, they both know that this attempt at finding their friend in a dark cave is going to be very dangerous. It will test both their courage and their loyalty to each other, and their determination to find their friend regardless of the hazards. Neither one has been in this kind of situation before, nor do they know just how they will react when their lives are on the line.

How they will respond and react to their coming ordeal, this test of valor; is something yet to be answered.

Now with the dynamite in one hand and his lighter in the other, Ethan looks at Joseph and taking a big breath of air says, "Here we go."

Acknowledging with a quick smile that conceals how very uneasy he is about this quest, a slight doubt begins to enter into Joseph's mind. Trying to think positive, but he knows the odds are against him and Ethan of ever coming back out of this cave alive. He grips the bear claw tightly, hoping to draw strength and spirit from it. He begins to feel a presence, and a strange sensation going through his body. Looking up, he sees an eagle high in the sky, its piercing call echoing for miles. Now determined and more confident, young Joseph stands tall, he will not wavier from this challenge, and he will not fail.

The two now step into the cave opening; and they walk a short distance before stopping. They must wait here, until their eyes adjust to the dark. Tensing up, they know that one of these beasts could be waiting just around the next corner. As their hearts begin beating faster and sweat now runs down their faces, they move deeper into the mine. Soon they are in total darkness and Ethan now is unable to see Joseph, who is standing right next to him. Reaching out Ethan grabs Joseph by his shoulder and the two now inch their way forward.

Now having second thoughts about moving around in the dark, Ethan speaks up suggesting, "Maybe we should have made some torches, to light the way, before coming in here."

Realizing he is right, "It's too late now," replies Joseph.

After a few more minutes, and still unable to see very well, they both decide that it is almost suicide to continue. Unable to see their hand in front of their faces, they know it will be impossible to defend themselves in here. With no way to see where they are going they could end up hopelessly lost and never find their way out.

However, once outside they can make a few torches as suggested before, and then they can return and try again. Now turning around, they begin to retrace their steps. This is a slow process, as they have gone around many corners. They stop several times, trying to decide which way to go, with nothing more than a guess to guide them. As the two have now stopped to rest again, they realize that they were too anxious in entering this cave without some sort of light. Their youth and over confidence in finding their friend may have doomed them.

Joseph tells Ethan, "When we get out of this tunnel, we should continue on our way to the camp, and then go to the nearest town and call the police."

Ethan doesn't want to leave, knowing that Chase is in here somewhere, but he is smart enough to know that he and Joseph are in way over their heads with this. Ethan agrees, saying, "Your right, with no weapons and no flashlights it is foolish for us to come in here."

As the two now begin to move along the tunnel wall, they suddenly can hear heavy breathing coming their way.

Ethan at once begins to panic, as his fear of enclosed places once again takes over. With his mind racing at the thought of encountering one of these beasts in this dark confined place, he grabs Joseph saying in a trembling voice, "What are we going to do?"

Joseph, who since he was a young boy, has been taught by his Grandfather, that it does no good to panic in dangerous situations. He now tells Ethan, "Calm down, get a hold of yourself Ethan."

Puzzled, Joseph doesn't understand why his friend has suddenly become so frightened. He knows how brave Ethan is, so this behavior surprises him. Joseph grabs Ethan and asks him, "What is wrong with you?"

Ethan, who by now has started shaking, tells him about his fear of enclosed places.

Joseph was unaware of his friend's condition, but he has heard of others who suffer from this same problem. Joseph assures his friend, "I will not abandon you, and we will get though this whole situation together."

It is obvious to Joseph now that Ethan is very scared, with his knees shaking and his breathing becoming very rapid.

Joseph says, "We'll slowly start backing up, let's not run."

At that very moment, they hear a loud thud noise, as if something very heavy has hit the floor. Listening, and trying not to make a sound, they know the noise is very close in front.

Before either knew what happened, Ethan has lit the fuse to the dynamite and he tosses it in front of them. Seeing the lit fuse Joseph immediately grabs Ethan, shoving him back and down onto the ground. Both lay still and cover their heads. They don't have to wonder any longer if the dynamite works or not. Because an explosion now shakes the ground and dirt begins falling down on them. They remain motionless until the dirt stops falling and they are sure it is safe. Now coughing from the dust in the air, they both listen for the heavy breathing that they had heard before. All is quiet, except for some dirt and rocks still falling here and there. Joseph roughly grabbing Ethan by the shirt tells him in an angry tone, "Don't do that again, you nearly got us killed."

Nearly beside himself with what he has just done, Ethan apologizes, "I'm sorry, but I panicked, and it won't happen again, I promise."

Still upset at his foolishness, "We can't stay here," answers Joseph, "we have to keep moving."

However, not knowing which way will lead them out; Joseph says, "We have to keep moving if we are going to find our way out."

Both young men now stand up, and using the wall as a guide they begin walking, hoping they are going in the right direction. Yet, at that moment, they again can hear the heavy breathing and it is much closer than it was before. Ethan, who has by now, gotten his anxiety under control, and speaking in a calm voice, says, "With this whole area so unstable, if I light one more stick of dynamite it might bring this mountain right down on top of us."

The two are in a very precarious situation, with the dynamite being their only weapon, it could also be their worst enemy, and seal them in this cave forever.

As the two scared, and confused young men stand next to each other, trying to figure a safe way out of here, all the while knowing that one of these beasts is very close. It is nerve racking not knowing what is going to happen next. They each know that together they stand a chance of surviving this ordeal, but if separated it could have tragic consequences. Ethan is about to say something, when he suddenly feels Joseph pull hard away from him, and Joseph is now screaming loudly, "Help me help me, the beast has me."

Ethan is trying his best to see in the darkness, he moves in the direction that he last heard Joseph calling him. He tries calling out to his friend, but the sound of Josephs voice is getting farther and farther away and soon he hears nothing. Ethan now crouches down, the cave is silent, and he is alone.

As his knees begin shaking and his breathing starts to increase, he knows it is only a matter of time before the beast comes back for him. His anxiety level is rising, and he puts his head in his hands, repeating the words "The only thing to fear is fear itself."

After several minutes, and having gotten control over his emotions, he grabs at the dynamite in his hand, knowing that if he lights one more it could cause a cave in. However, he also knows that the Shadow Beast will soon return for him, and its revenge, he believes could be much worse than being buried alive.

He realizes he is caught in a terrible situation, one that he isn't prepared to be in. Having no knowledge of mines, and without supplies, young Ethan Miller must come to terms with the fact that he is going to die. Sitting on the floor of this tunnel, he thinks about his family, and he did want to see them again. Now with a determined and serious look on his face, and fists clenched tight, he gets up and begins walking as he moves his hands across the tunnel wall. He has decided that this will not be his final resting place, no matter what lies ahead he is going to meet it head on. Ethan now feels a surge of courage and confidents in himself he never knew he had. Slowly he inches his way around several corners and to his surprise, he can see a light in the distance. A way out he believes, but as he gets closer to the light, it becomes apparent to him that it isn't coming from the outside.

Now he moves with great caution, trying to figure out what this light source is coming from. Soon, he can see that the light is coming from a side chamber just up ahead.

Ethan is now about twenty yards from the lighted chamber, thinking that Joseph is in there and somehow a rescue team has come to help them.

He calls out, "Are you in there Joseph?" Just as he is reaching the entrance to this lighted chamber, another tremor shakes the area.

This tremor is much stronger that the last one and it also lasts longer. Ethan is now falling backwards, and trying his best to regain his balance. Large sections of the ceiling are now falling all around him. As he staggers forward trying to make it to the chamber, the tunnel ceiling directly in front of him abruptly collapses. Ethan turns around and begins running, the dust is now very thick, and while trying to cover his mouth he trips and falls, with his head landing hard on the ground.

He lay motionless for several hours, alone and trapped deep within the mountain. Realizing that he was unconscious, Ethan opens his eyes again, he is still in total darkness, but he is grateful to be still alive. He can tell that his body is covered with dirt and small rocks, and several large boulders are on his legs. When he tries moving these large boulders, he feels a sharp pain in his right leg. Pushing some of the smaller rocks off his legs, he is able to free his left leg, but his right leg is under a large boulder, but as much as he tries, he can't move it.

He knows he is in a bad situation, and he has to think hard and fast if he is going to survive. He now begins to try to dig under the boulder with his hands, hoping to create a large enough space to be able to pull his injured leg free. However, he soon realizes that the ground is just too hard, no way is he going to dig in this rocky ground. Leaning back as he rubs his hand across his face, and now beginning to come to grips with just how dire the situation is. Ethan knows with his leg trapped, and no tools to dig himself out with, and his air supply running low, that this is it. He now tells himself that he has run out of miracles, there just is nothing left to do but lie down and die.

After several minutes of feeling sorry for himself, Ethan grabs the sticks of dynamite in his belt. He knows that these sticks have the power to move this boulder off his leg, but the question is how much of his leg will be left afterwards. He pulls the lighter from his pocket; his next action could very well kill him. Ethan thinks about the odds of surviving the explosion, knowing that even if the blast does move the boulder off his leg, he is sure the cave will collapse on top of him. This is a no win situation for him, and after agonizing about it for a long time, he decides to light the stick of dynamite, and stop prolonging the inevitable.

Ethan once again bows his head, and says a short prayer. With tears running down his face, he holds up the dynamite in one hand and the lighter in the other. He doesn't want to die, and realizing that only a miracle can save him now. As he is bringing the dynamite and the lighter closer together, he is surprised to see the boulder begin to move.

Ethan lets out a big sigh of relief, thinking that Joseph has somehow found Chase and he is alive, and now the two of them are moving this boulder to rescue him. Putting the dynamite down he holds the lighter up in the air, with a scream of pain as the boulder rolls off his leg he calls out, "Thank god you guys got here when you did, another ten seconds and I would have blown this place up."

As Ethan holds the lighter out in front of him to see his friends, he is nearly shocked into fainting when two hairy arms reach for him. Unable to move, he stares in disbelief, as they roughly grab him by the legs. His head is jerked back as he is quickly pulled across the ground. The pain from his broken leg is too much and Ethan begins to go into shock. The Shadow Beast now drags Ethan down a long narrow tunnel, Ethan's eyes stare straight ahead, and his arms dangle freely at his sides. The next thing Ethan knows is that he is being thrown down onto a chamber floor. Looking up through blurred vision, he can see light shining in from a hole in the ceiling. Lying there on the ground, he is so scared that he can't move. With the pain in his right leg causing him to nearly black out, he struggles to stay conscious.

The quick successions of events in the last few minutes have been too much for him to comprehend. His head spinning, and mind wondering, he struggles to separate reality from illusion. Suddenly he can hear a voice, "Are you alright?"

Dazed and bewildered, now looking around in the semi darkness, it takes his eyes a few seconds to get focused. He reaches out with his hand and is surprised when he touches someone's face. In a shaky voice he asks, "Who are you?"

Joseph speaks up saying, "It's me Ethan, don't you recognize me."

After a moment, it is clear to Joseph that his friend is in shock and he can see that Ethan's leg is bent at an awkward position. Joseph removes his jacket and lays it on Ethan. Propping up Ethan's head he asks, "What happened to you, can you tell me what happened to you?" However, Ethan doesn't answer, instead he tries rolling up into a ball, and starts crying. Joseph knows that Ethan must have been through a terrible ordeal, he comforts his friend telling him, "Everything is going to be all right."

Joseph knows that the Shadow Beast is nearby; he can occasionally hear its heavy breathing.

He also understands that going back through the tunnel will be impossible, besides he won't leave his friend here alone. Glancing up, he begins to examine the large hole in the ceiling. The opening is about ten feet from the ground, and it measures about twenty feet across. If he can somehow reach it, then he can escape and make it back to the nearest town and get help.

However, reaching it is going to be a problem, looking around there is nothing to use for a ladder.

Getting up and walking over until he is directly under this hole, Joseph tries jumping up to reach the opening, but he falls just short. He is not going to give up, his life and the lives of his friends, depends on him getting out of here and finding help. Now Joseph sits back down on the floor of this chamber, trying to think of any way possible to reach that opening.

Looking around he sees many bones scattered about, at first thinking, they are just animal bones, until he sees a human skull. A sick feeling is now in his stomach. He knows now for sure that these Shadow Beasts do eat people. After composing himself he reaches out and picks up a large bone, it appears to be a leg bone. He breaks off one end, leaving a sharp point, this he can use as a weapon. Setting down his new weapon, he must concentrate on first trying to escape.

One idea he has is to tie his pants and shirt together, and on one end, he ties a piece of wood. He hopes to throw this up through the opening and to try to snag it on a jagged rock nearby.

Once this is secured, he then will pull himself up through the opening. But time after time, each attempt fails, after tossing his homemade rope through the hole, when he pulls on it, the piece of wood would come falling back towards him. Getting very frustrated, he begins cursing and kicking the walls. He now hears Ethan call for him in a faint voice, and he very rapidly rushes to his side. Kneeling down and lifting up Ethan's head, he cradles his friend on his lap. He now thinks that this is going to be a terrible way to die. Joseph tries calming down his friend by telling him, "Do you know how much fun we will have once we get back to the campus."

Ethan pats Joseph on the shoulder; trying to speak, but his words are slurred. Joseph tells him, "Just rest, I'll figure a way out of here."

To his horror, the Shadow Beast suddenly burst into the chamber, and it knocks him to the ground. It now grabs Ethan, and with its mouth open and its teeth showing, it is very obvious to Joseph that this beast is going to eat Ethan. No way is he going to just sit and do nothing. With more courage than he thought he had, he jumps to his feet and charges at the beast.

But with one swing of its mighty arm the beast easily knocks Joseph backwards and into the far wall. He lands hard, but not deterred by this he gets to his feet again, and picking up several rocks he starts throwing them at the beast. Walking right up to it, Joseph shows no fear. Again, the beast hits Joseph causing him to fall back and onto the ground. This time Joseph is a little slower getting up, and blood is now running down his face from a cut around his right eye. Dizzy and on wobbly legs, he again charges at the beast. This time he manages to duck under the beasts arm and he runs right into it. The Shadow Beast lets out a roar and grabbing Joseph by his shoulders picks him up off the ground and violently shakes him. Joseph now feels as if his limbs are being torn right from his body, and again he is thrown across the room. Landing with a sickening crunch as he hits the rock wall, Joseph clenches his teeth in pain, the blood beginning to flow freely down his face. He rolls onto his side while coughing up blood, and looking across the room, he sees the beast reaching once more for Ethan. Undeterred by the pain he is feeling, once more Joseph summons up the strength and fortitude to get to his feet. He is now limping badly on one leg, and is unable see out of his left eye, also he has a shooting pain in his back making it very difficult to stand upright.

Nevertheless, Joseph Browndeer will not quit, he will fight with every ounce of strength he has left in his bruised and battered body. He repeats to himself, "I' am a member of the Yakama Tribe, we are warriors and men of honor who don't know the word defeat, and most important, I'm the Grandson of Kicking Bear."

Moving much slower now, and shaking his head trying to clear his vision, he looks up to see the beast opening its mouth, it has Ethan's foot in its grip and is about to bite it. Joseph now staggers forward then falls to the ground, he begins yelling, but the beast pays no attention to him. With severe pain now shooting through his body, Joseph franticly tries to get to his feet, while doing so his hand touches the splintered bone he had made earlier.

He closes his eyes for a second, and summoning up the spirits of his ancestors, Joseph calls on them to help him.

Opening his eyes and looking at the beast, Joseph begins to smile; he feels he is no longer alone. Suddenly and like magic, in the corner he can see a white glow, and emerging from this is the Ghost Warrior. It is the one that he had seen earlier, with its hair and feathers moving as if they are blowing in the wind, and the pure white horse rearing up on two legs. This Ghost warrior with its mesmerizing stare, points its staff at the beast. Feeling a surge of adrenalin rush through his body, Joseph knows what to do. With one last heroic effort, Joseph lunges at the beast, driving the point of the jagged bone into its upper thigh.

The Shadow Beast lets go of Ethan and roars so loud that Joseph thinks it is going to cause a cave in. With anger in its eyes, the beast takes one last swing at Joseph, catching him in the right shoulder. As the mighty arm comes down, Joseph can feel bones in his shoulder breaking. Crying out in pain; he is spun around, where he then falls to the ground. The beasts turns, and runs out of the chamber, still roaring in pain.

Joseph now is screaming in pain himself, as he clutches his shoulder, lying on his back kicking his legs. Biting down hard, the pain is more intense than he has ever felt in his life. After several minutes of nearly blacking out, the pain begins to subside. Beginning to calm down, he must stay focused; he knows that the Shadow Beast has only suffered a minor wound, and that it will be back.

On the verge of passing out every time he moves, Joseph slowly manages to inch his way over to Ethan, all the while clinching his teeth in pain. He has never suffered so much hurt in his life, and the situation looks bleak. Finally making it over to his friend, Joseph closes his eyes.

Ethan reaches out his hand, touching Joseph on the head. The two friends sit in this lonely chamber of nightmares, hoping for a miracle, but expecting nothing less than a cruel ending to their lives.

Joseph now begins to chant a song taught to him by his Grandfather. In this song, it asks the Great Spirit to forgive him for any wrong he may have done, and to release his spirit so that he may meet his ancestors.

As Joseph is singing and moving his head, Ethan touches his arm and asks, "What is that?"

Joseph stops and replies, "What are you looking at?"

Ethan then points at the hole in the ceiling.

Joseph turns his head upwards, and blinks his eyes several times, looking through the blood that now covers his face, he tilts his head up at the hole.

A look of complete exhilaration is on his face now, and with a shaking hand, he covers his mouth. He can see perched on the edge of the hole is an eagle, and it is looking down at the two wounded young men. Through sheer determination and will power, Joseph manages to get up on one elbow. Looking at this good omen, he now feels that maybe the predicament he's in may turn out all right after all.

"Everything is going to be all right, this eagle is a sign that help is on the way."

The eagle now lets out a loud cry, which echoes throughout the chamber, and then it majestically flies away. After seeing this, Joseph lies back down, calmness is on his face, and he closes his eyes. He is thinking that at any moment he will see members of his tribe coming in to rescue him and Ethan. He tells himself "I have beaten the Shadow Beast, and members of my tribe will now look upon me as a great warrior."

However, his over confidence is shattered when he can hear the familiar footsteps of the beast walking down the tunnel. It is still roaring loudly, and Joseph knows that it is coming for him now.

Trying desperately to find anything to defend himself with, but all that is around is a few rocks and bones. Ethan now tries sitting up, and looking at Joseph, he can see how battered his friend is.

Still in shock himself, he tells Joseph, "If you can walk you need to try to find a way out of here, don't worry about me, save yourself."

Joseph looks at his friend, whom he has not known all that long, yet this stranger has helped him fight those bullies back on the campus. He stayed in that field to fight the bear while telling him to run to the safety of the minors shack. "No," he tells himself, "I will not abandon this friend of mine."

Joseph tells Ethan, "I will not leave; I will stay with you no matter what happens."

All Ethan can do is reach out his hand, touching Joseph on the knee and saying, "Your grandfather will be so proud of you when he hears how you stayed by my side."

Joseph replies, "That is if we make it out of here alive."

Ethan now sitting with his back against the wall replies, "You told me that members of your tribe don't know the word defeat."

With a determined look on his face and eyes focused, Joseph answers, "You are right; we will make it out of here, and that I promise."

As the two now talk of the stories they will tell once they get back to the campus, a large shadow blocks the entrance to the chamber. Both know that the Shadow Beast has returned, and by the sound of its heavy breathing, that it is back seeking revenge.

Joseph yells as best he can, "You will not kill us, go away."

However, the beast has other plans and it quickly rushes over and grabs Joseph by the leg, dragging him across the floor. With so many injuries Joseph is helpless to defend himself, all he can do is to put up a puny resistance. Again and again he is thrown hard to the ground, and he now is trying desperately to catch his breath. Now with its victim lying helpless on the ground the Shadow Beast begins to walk back and forth. Joseph doesn't understand why it doesn't kill him right away. Suddenly the beast reaches down and picking up Joseph again, it throws him back over next to Ethan. Landing hard Joseph withers in pain, and he tries crawling away but the creature again grabs him and it tosses him back across the room. Hitting and rolling several times, Joseph now knows that this beast is torturing him first, before it will eventfully kill and eat him.

Unable to put up any resistance to this madness, he continues to try to crawl away, only to be picked up and tossed about like a rag doll. Joseph is on the verge of passing out, his whole body feels numb, this he knows is a sign that he is going into shock. With unwavering determination and grit, Joseph Browndeer, Grandson of Kicking Bear, will never give up.

As he is lying on the floor waiting for the creature to grab him once more, his hand touches something in his pocket. Reaching in, he pulls out the bear's claw, the one that the medicine man in his tribe has blessed. The one item to remind him of his native heritage, he has always carried this with him. Joseph takes several deep breaths and calls for the creature to come and get him.

Ethan now hearing his friend say this, knows that the end is near and he desperately tries to think of what he can do. At that moment, Ethan sees the stick of dynamite in his belt, pulling it out and holding it in his trembling hands, "This" he utters "will end this whole nightmare."

He looks at the beast who now has Joseph held in the air by one leg staring him in the face. Ethan must decide quickly what to do; he knows once the creature is finished with Joseph that it will come for him.

He decides to light the dynamite and put an end to this, the explosion will cause a cave in killing all of them. Just as Ethan lights the fuse, Joseph grips the bears claw, and with what strength he has left, he jabs it into the beasts left eye. The Shadow Beast releases Joseph and holding its hand over its injured eye starts roaring in pain, it backs up to the cave entrance.

"This," Ethan cries, "is the miracle that they have been waiting for," and he tosses the lit dynamite towards the beast and calls to Joseph, "Cover yourself up!"

In a matter of seconds, the explosion rocks the ground and large parts of the ceiling are now crashing down around them. The noise is deafening, causing his ears to ring and his head is pounding. After several minutes of remaining motionless, Ethan begins wiping the dirt off himself, surprised that he is still alive. Coughing from the dust in the air, he looks around trying to find his friend, but he sees no movement.

He now lays his head down, a tear rolls down his face, he had liked Joseph, and he had considered him a good man. As Ethan now lies on his back staring at the partly collapsed ceiling, wondering if the explosion has killed the Shadow Beast, or is it just wounded. After several attempts at trying to get up fail, he is startled to hear movement not far away. His heart starts beating faster now, and trying desperately to think of what to do when this creature comes for him. Ethan looks through the dust-filled room and he now hears coughing. With a tone of excitement in his voice, he calls out for his friend. "Joseph, Joseph!"

Joseph picks up his head and shacks off the dirt, and looking over at Ethan he manages to wave his hand. Ethan is elated that Joseph is alive and tells him, "I thought you were dead?"

After coughing several times, Joseph replies, "You didn't think that ole Shadow Beast was going to get the best of me did you."

With joy in their laughter, they both begin crawling towards each other. With suffering intense pain, both continue their slow advance towards one another, and when they meet neither one can believe the other is alive. Ethan gives Joseph a big hug, but quickly lets him go when he yells in pain. Both having multiple broken bones and cuts all over their bodies, they lean against one another.

"We shall wait," says Joseph, "I have seen a vision sent from the Great Spirit, we will all make it out of here alive."

Forcing a smile, Ethan replies, "I hope you are right my friend, I hope you are right."

With sheer willpower, and fighting the dizziness and pain, trying to stay awake, Ethan asks, "What of the Shadow Beast, is it dead?

Wiping blood and dirt from his face, "I have no doubt," answers Joseph, "the explosion must have blown it to pieces."

Unknown to the two young men lying on the chamber floor, the Shadow Beast isn't dead. The explosion only blown it out into the tunnel, where it is buried under a pile rocks and dirt. As the two injured friends wait to be rescued, a large hairy hand begins to twitch from under a mountain of rubble not far away.

CHAPTER 12

With the Shadow Beasts leading the way, Chase is surprised at how fast they move. He and the Professor must run several times just to keep up with them. Shortly thereafter, they emerge out into the daylight; grateful to be out of the tunnel.

Walking over to a large outcropping of rocks, they watch the Shadow Beasts gently lay the smaller one down onto the ground. The three Shadow Beasts stay very near the little one, and they softly stroke its fur.

Looking across a barren landscape, Chase can see the forest not far away. Turning around the huge mountain rises up sharply behind him.

The Professor tells him, "You will stay here until I can find a safe place for them in the woods."

As the Professor starts walking away, an uneasy and apprehensive Chase calls to him asking, "You're not going to leave me here alone with these creatures are you?"

Turning around, the Professor calls back to Chase saying, "You are perfectly safe, there's nothing to worry about."

Chase still feels jittery around these giant creatures, and as he begins running to catch up to the Professor, another tremor shakes the ground. Both men lose their balance and fall to the ground, with Chase sliding down a flat surface towards a steep gorge. Desperately grabbing at the ground, he is unable to stop himself. His momentum takes him right over the edge; where he is now hanging off a ledge. He looks down and sees that it is about a forty-five foot drop to the ground below. He knows a fall from this height will not kill him, but nonetheless he still would rather avoid the fall. Chase desperately grabs onto the loose rock, hoping to avoid finding out just how bad he will be hurt when he hits the ground below. The Professor is slow at getting to his feet and he is a considerable distance from Chase, he calls for Chase to hang on. Just as Chase loses his grip and begins falling back, a large fury hand reaches down and grabs him by the arm. Looking up in surprise, Chase is staring right into the eyes of one of the Shadow Beasts. Without hesitation, the beast easily lifts Chase up and gently sets him down. Speechless, Chase gazes wide eyed at his rescuer, and watches as it now goes back over to join the others of its kind.

The Professor arrives and asks, "Are you alright?"

Still stunned, Chase looks up and replies, "I' am, thanks to that," and he stops and asks, "Just what is that one's name?"

With a smile, the Professor answers, "his name is Kajika."

Waving his hand at the beast, Chase says, "I owe Kajika a big thank you for saving my life."

The Professor tells him, "Later I will show you the sign language for thank you, but right now, it is important that we find a safe place to hide these creatures."

Hoping to avoid any more delays, he now asks Chase, "Do you still feel uncomfortable staying here with these animals?"

Shaking his head, Chase replies, "After what just happened, I know they won't hurt me."

The Professor then says, "I will be back soon."

He now begins his decent into the raven not far away, and from there it leads into the forest. Chase walks back over and is now sitting down only an arm's length from the Shadow Beasts.

Not knowing what to say or do, he waves his hand in the air and says, "Hello."

One of the Shadow Beasts gets up and begins making a grunting sound, Chase has no clue as what this means. Therefore, he backs up just a bit, and he watches as the female begins stroking the fur of the small one that is injured. These creatures show compassion and sympathy for each other, this has Chase wondering just how far from humans are these creatures. Maybe, he thinks, they could be the missing link, the part of our ancestral tree that is absent.

As he gets up the nerve to reach out and touch one of these creatures he suddenly can hear an explosion, and the ground shakes. The Shadow Beasts are now moving around and waving their arms in the air. Chase knows that that explosion was manmade, letting him know that other people are around here. He can see that not far away dust is rising up, and wonders why someone would be using dynamite around this old abandoned mine. His first priority, however, is to calm down these creatures. With a relaxed composure on his face, he stands in front of them and motions with his hands for them to sit down. He tries talking in a quiet voice saying, "It will be alright, it will be alright."

The creatures look at Chase and to his surprise; they slowly start to calm down. Within minutes, they have sat back down and they stare at Chase who now begins talking to them just as if they were people. He knows they don't understand what he is saying, but that it is the tone of his voice and the way he is talking that assures them that things are fine now. Chase is relieved, if these giant creatures wanted to pick him up and throw him off the cliff, there is nothing he can do to stop them.

Now looking over to where the dust is rising into the sky, Chase begins walking across the rocks and after climbing a small ridge, he can see a large hole in the ground. The dust is filtering up from here, and he now creeps across the rocky surface to get closer. Realizing, however that the ground around here maybe unstable, so he decides to get down on his hands and knees and slowly inches his way forward. Now just a few feet from the hole he calls out, "Can anybody hear me?" After a moment of silence, he can hear a very faint voice, and it is almost unrecognizable.

Chase waits a moment, now yells, "Is that you Joseph."

To his surprise, he hears Joseph reply, "We are down here."

Chase inches right up to the edge of the hole and looking down through the dust; he can see Joseph and Ethan. With excitement in his voice he calls out, "It sure is good to see you guys."

In-between coughs, Joseph replies, "Ethan and I both need medical help, and neither one of us can walk."

Excited, Chase now motions with his hand and says, "Don't worry I'll get help, just stay put."

Chase now hurries back towards the forest, trying desperately to locate the Professor.

Joseph shakes Ethan gently on the shoulder, telling him, "Chase is going to get help; we are going to be rescued."

However, his friend doesn't reply, Ethan has slipped into a coma. Joseph is himself fighting the effects of his injuries, he keeps blacking out, and the cut on his head continues to bleed.

Chase has made his way down from the rocks, and is standing at the edge of the forest and begins calling for the Professor.

He knows that every minute that passes is critical, his friends need medical help immediately. After several agonizing minutes, he soon spots the Professor, and he starts waving his arms, motioning for him to come over by him. When the Professor sees Chase waving his arms, he begins running in his direction. Soon he is next to Chase, who tells him of his two friends down in the chamber. The two now race over and calling down into the hole, they get no reply. Chase desperately is seeking a way to get down by his friends. Worried and anxious, he paces back and forth, finally shouting, "We have to get down there."

After looking over the situation, the Professor replies, "I have some rope back at my shack, but it will take time to go there and come back."

Throwing his arms into the air, "We don't have any time to waste," franticly replies Chase, "we need to get them out of there now."

Standing up and looking around, Chase scans the surrounding area trying to find anything that he can use to get down in that hole. With a look of panic on his face, Chase feels helpless, unable to reach his friends.

The Professor tells him, "I will go and get the rope; we have no other way of getting down to them."

Chase suddenly sees something in the woods and his eyes get big. He yells to the Professor, "Just wait a minute, I have an idea." Chase now runs to the edge of the woods and hanging from a tree, he sees several long vines. He calls back saying, "These long vines will work just fine."

Making his way into the woods, Chase climbs up the tree and pulling his knife from his pocket, he cuts several vines.

Swiftly climbing back down, and once on the ground he quickly picks up the vines and carries them hurriedly back to the hole in the ground.

Smiling, the Professor says, "Good idea young man; now let's tie one end around this boulder."

The two work as fast as they can, and after having secured the vine, Chase begins climbing down. Once on the ground he gives his eyes a moment to adjust to the low light. He now can see his two friends lying on the ground and he hurries over to them. Getting down on his knees, it's quickly apparent to him, just how severe their injuries are.

He can see the cut above Josephs right eye, the blood is flowing freely down his face. Knowing from his medical experience that the first thing he needs to do is to stop the bleeding. Chase pulls out his knife and cuts the sleeve from his shirt. Next, he wraps it tightly around Josephs head, and applies pressure. While doing this he can see that Ethan's right leg is bent at an odd angle, suggesting that it is broken.

Chase now tries getting a response from Joseph, but his body is limp, a small amount blood is coming from his mouth. Hearing his shallow breathing, he puts his head on Joseph's chest. With his shallow breathing, Chase now realizes that Joseph has a collapsed lung. Knowing the damage that could occur if he tries to move Joseph, the situation is now serious.

Chase now calls back up telling the Professor, "It may not be a good idea to move them, we could cause even more damage if we try moving them out of here."

"I'm coming down to have a look for myself."

At that instant, another tremor shakes the ground. Chase quickly puts his body over his injured friends, as more of the ceiling falls. When the tremor stops, Chase coughs from the dust in the air. Realizing how unstable this area is, it causes Chase to change his mind. He yells back to the Professor telling him, "It is just too dangerous to leave my friends in here, this place can collapse at any time."

Chase gently pulls Joseph over until he is now directly beneath the hole. He ties the vine around Joseph's waist, and tells the Professor, "Start pulling up, but be gentle."

A little at a time, Joseph is pulled up through the opening, and once on top the Professor unties the vine and lowers it back down. Now Chase does the same to Ethan, who is also unconscious, he too is pulled up through the hole to safety. As Chase is waiting for the Professor to lower the vine, he hears a noise coming from the tunnel. Wondering what it could be he calls up asking, "Do you know if there is anyone else around here?"

Before the Professor can answer, Joseph who has now regained consciousness replies, "A Shadow Beast had nearly killed me and Ethan, and it is in the tunnel, but we blew it to pieces."

Chase slowly walks towards the tunnel and looking to his right he can see a hairy arm moving in the rubble, this one Shadow Beast, he knows must be the Cannibal Demon. Without haste he quickly runs back to the center of the chamber and looking up through the hole, he yells "I don't think the Shadow Beast is dead; now get me out of here."

The vine is again lowered down quickly, and grabbing it, Chase begins climbing up. Stopping once, he looks over and there in the doorway he can see the outline of the beast. He continues climbing, and once on top he tells Joseph and the Professor that they need to get out of here fast.

A loud roar echoing from the chamber below, can now be heard. The Professor says, "We can't move these men with their injuries, it will be too risky."

Very upset and disturbed by these recent turn of events, Chase franticly replies, "We can't stay here, the beast will find its way out of the tunnel and come after us."

The Professor says, "I have a radio stored in my shed along with other supplies not far from here."

With a demanding voice, he tells Chase, "You will stay here and I will go and call for a medical chopper. It should arrive in less than thirty minutes; I also have a rifle there."

Chase reluctantly agrees, hoping that help arrives before the beast manages to find its way out of the tunnel and it comes up here. He now watches as the Professor moves down from the rocks and enters the forest. Joseph's condition has by now stabilized, and after gaining consciousness, he manages to lean himself up against a boulder. Chase is doing his best to comfort his friend. Sitting beside him, he tries wiping some of the blood from his face. Joseph can barely hold his head up, his breathing is shallow and his skin is cold and damp.

As Joseph Looks over to his right, what he sees causes him to shake. Grabbing Chase by the arm and in an excited voice utters, "They are going to eat us."

Chase now realizing what his friend is looking at, reassures him that these Shadow Beasts are friendly, "They won't hurt us, they are friendly, trust me."

Chase now begins telling Joseph everything about the Professor, and that he has been studying these creatures for years.

He tells Joseph, "Only one of these Shadow Beasts kills people, and that one beast is down in the chamber."

Relieved, Joseph replies, "Then we are safe, because we blew it up with the dynamite."

Shaking his head, Chase replies, "That explosion didn't kill the beast, it is still alive."

With a dejected look, Joseph bows his head down.

"However," Chase says "The Professor has gone to radio for help, and soon we'll all be out of here."

Coughing and holding his hand over his mouth, Joseph looks up at Chase and says, "I hope the help arrives before that Shadow Beast finds it's way to us."

Trying to keep a positive attitude, and reassure his friend, "Don't worry," replies Chase as he fixes the bandage on Joseph's head, "everything is going to be alright."

Feeling that his friend should know everything; "In addition," Chase speaks up, "your Grandfather has been helping the Professor all these years."

Joseph, upon hearing this looks down and mutters, "Why did he not tell me?"

Right then a look of regret crosses his face, and he suddenly knows the answer to that question. It is because he has ignored everything that his grandfather has tried teaching him. Joseph had wanted nothing to do with stories of Shadow Beasts, spirits, and ghosts. He did not want to learn the ways of his ancestors. He had tried to adapt to the ways of the white man, and now Joseph Browndeer, lowered his head, he is ashamed of what he has done.

He wonders if his grandfather will forgive him, and will his tribe accept him back.

Chase is now taking a closer look at Ethan's broken leg. He now begins setting it straight, and with one hard pull; the broken bone is set straight. He is thankful that Ethan is still unconscious; the pain would have been almost unbearable. Next Chase puts a stick alongside the broken leg, and wraps the vine tightly around it, "This should keep it in place," he says.

Chase now turns back to Joseph and says, "Let me have a look at that cut on your head."

At that very moment, Joseph gets a look of fear on his face and franticly starts pointing at something behind Chase. In a frightened voice, Joseph says, "We don't have time for that." Turning around Chase is startled to see the rouge Shadow Beast emerging from a steep raven, and it starts coming their way. They can see that the beast is injured; as it limps, it also holds its left hand down next to its hip. These injuries, they know are no doubt the results of the explosion. Now, with its face distorted in anger, and roaring loudly, it continues approaching them. Franticly Chase begins looking around for anything to use as a weapon, but he is defenseless.

Quickly assessing the situation, Joseph tells Chase, "Run and save himself, it's too late for me and Ethan."

Chase slowly backs up as he watches the Shadow Beast methodically advance towards him.

Joseph now begins chanting the death song of his people, this lonely and barren piece of rock he believes is where he is going to die.

Chase now must decide if he is going to run and save his own life or if he will stay and face death with his two companions. Chase looks down at his two friends; they are good people he tells himself. They would not abandon him in this situation if he were the one lying on the ground and unable to move. Therefore, Chase steps between the beast and his friends, knowing full well that he is no match for this huge beast. He will not run away, and with knees shaking, heart racing, and sweat beginning to run down his face, young Chase Watkins has chosen honor and death over betrayal and life.

The injured and mad beast steadily keeps coming closer; partially dragging its right foot, and constantly wiping with its hand at what remains of its left eye.

Chase stands straight and doubles up his fists, trying his best to get into a good defensive posture. Just how he is going to fight this creature he doesn't know, but fight it he will. The thought of this creature first tearing him to pieces, and then attacking his helpless friends, has him very angry. Gritting his teeth, he decides that attacking the creature first may give him a slight advantage. Now facing a certain death, he prepares to charge straight ahead when he hears a noise from behind him.

Relieved that the Professor has returned, he calls back over his shoulder, "You got here just in time Professor."

After getting no answer, he turns his head and there standing not more than five feet away is another Shadow Beast, he quickly recognizes it as Kajika.

Chase now finds himself trapped between these two beasts as they begin to roar back and forth. Then in the blink of an eye, he sees Kajika race by him and it jumps at the rogue Shadow Beast. The two huge beasts now begin fighting and rolling around on the ground. They kick dust and dirt up into the air, as both try to gain advantage over the other.

Chase stares in wide-eyed astonishment at this battle royal. Several minutes pass as each one of these beasts delivers horrific blows to the other. Finally, and to Chase's horror, he sees the rouge beast get to its feet. It momentarily stares at Chase, baring its teeth, and swinging it head from side to side. Saddened as Kajika lays motionless on the ground,

Staring back at the beast, Chase is hoping that it has had enough. With its injuries it must be in a great deal of pain, he is positive that it will turn and run away.

This small flicker of hope quickly disappears, when the rogue beast begins walking towards him.

Swallowing hard and in disbelief, Chase again stands next to his friends.

"This," he says to himself, "is surely the end. With no weapon to defend myself with, this beast will kill me very quickly."

However, he does have his small pocketknife, it won't inflict much damage he knows, but at least he'll go down fighting. Now pulling the knife out and pointing it straight, young Chase again faces the beast alone. The rouge beast now begins raising its arms in the air and swinging its head back and forth, as it senses that Chase will be an easy victim.

Chases heart skips a beat when he sees Kajika begin to move. At first fearing that it was dead, but now watching as it rolls to its side, he has hope again. Startled when he sees it get to its feet and charge right at the rouge beast. The momentum of Kajika slamming into the rouge beast takes both beasts right over the edge and down into the raven. Chase races to the edge and looking down he can see one beast not moving, its head shattered by the rock that it landed on. The other beast, groaning loudly, is now trying desperately to get to its feet. Chase is now momentarily frozen, at first he doesn't know which beast is which. Straining his eyes, he suddenly can see the familiar gray patch of fur on the Shadow Beast that is still alive. He knows it is Kajika, and a wave of relief and joy comes over him.

Thankful for this, he lets out a big sigh of relief, and turning around he sees the Professor in the distance.

Chase now goes over to check on his friends, and when the Professor arrives, he tells him how Kajika saved his life.

The two go over to the edge of the raven and they can see the other two Shadow Beasts have gone down into the raven, and they are helping Kajika, it is an amazing sight. Chase speaks up saying, "I would not believe this unless I had seen it with my own eyes."

The Professor tells Chase, "I was able to contact the nearest hospital and they should be here in thirty minutes."

"Now" he says, "we need to hide the body of the rogue Shadow Beast, no one can know of their existence."

Looking at Chase, the Professor now asks, "Can I have your word that you won't tell anyone about these remarkable animals?"

Chase smiles and replies, "I owe them for saving my life, not once but twice, and I will do whatever I can to protect them."

Patting him on the back, "Good" replies the Professor, "first we need to hide the body of the dead one."

Both men now make their way down into the raven only to realize that the beast is too heavy for them to move. The Professor again repeats, "No one else must know about these creatures, we have to do something before the helicopter gets here."

Chase suggests, "Why don't we simply bury the beast, using the rocks all around us."

Again, the Professor remarks that Chase has had a good idea. Now the two begin pilling rocks on the creature and just as they are finishing they begin to hear the sound of the chopper. The two now hurry up the steep bank and once they reach their two injured friends on the ground, the Professor lights a flare, making it easier for the chopper pilot to find their location.

Within minutes the chopper lands and several medics race over and begin treating Joseph and Ethan. Once the two injured men are secured onto the stretchers, they are then quickly taken back to the helicopter. Within minutes, the chopper lifts off the ground and is soon heading for the nearest hospital.

Chase asks the Professor, "What did you tell the medics before they got here, I know that they would want to know the cause of the injuries?"

The Professor answers, "I simply told them that two hikers had fallen off a cliff and were in serious trouble."

The two now sit, reflecting on the events of the last few hours, it had been quite the adventure. Suddenly the Professor jumps up, and looking across the rocks he says, "Where are the other Shadow Beasts?"

Chase now joins the Professor as they both hurry over and looking around; the Shadow Beasts are nowhere to be seen.

Chase asks, "Where could they have gone, did they go back into the mines when they heard the chopper coming?"

"No" replies the professor, "They are too smart to do that, but there is one place that they may have gone."

Chase and the Professor, must first go to the shack and pick up several flashlights. After doing this, and with the Professor leading the way, they go deep into the forest. Traveling several miles, they are at last standing at the entrance to a cave.

The Professor says, "If the Shadow Beasts have gone anywhere, it will be here."

Looking like an ordinary cave to him, Chase asks, "What makes this cave so special?"

Waving his hand, "Just follow me," answers the professor "and you will see."

Ducking their heads to avoid the overhanging tree branches, the two quietly enter the cave. Shining their lights around they quickly find the Shadow Beasts. Chase is surprised that they coward to the back of the cave, such big animals should be afraid of nothing.

The Professor says, "These creatures are naturally very shy and timid and they want nothing to do with people. That," he says, "is why these creatures are very rarely seen by anyone." The Professor gently touches their fur and they touch him back. It reminds Chase of a meeting between old friends.

Chase examines further the inside of this cave, and he can now see a feathered headdress hanging on the wall, under it are several bows and a quiver of arrows. His light continues to scan the cave, he can see a pair moccasins and a spear.

He has to catch his breath when he sees a large skeleton lying on a wooden table. The Professor seeing Chase upset comes over to him saying, "This is an old Indian burial mound."

Chase points to the large skeleton, and asks, "What is that?

The professor replies, "It is the remains of a Shadow Beast. The Indians must have put its body in here long ago, and how it died, I don't know but these creatures have always been regarded by the Native Indians as supernatural. They are in all the stories told from one generation to another."

He continues, "These creatures often come here when they feel threatened. As long as they remain here they will be safe."

He tells Chase, "Now that we know the Shadow Beasts are safe, we need to get to the hospital to check on your friends."

The two leave the cave and hurry from the forest, and when they arrive back at the Professor's shack, he surprises Chase by bringing out a four-wheeler. Noticing that wide-eyed expression on Chases face again, the Professor replies, "You didn't think that I walked from here to the road did you."

Both begin to laugh and the professor motions for Chase to get on. They waste no time and once they reach the dead end road, the Professor goes over by several large bushes and begins pulling tree branches off a large pile. To Chase's surprise, a car is hid under all that brush. The Professor says, "I had to hide my car so no one would know that I was in these woods."

Chase can see Ethan's car, but not having the keys to it does him no good.

The drive to the hospital takes three hours, and once there, Chase rushes in the front door. Asking at the front deck about his friends, he is told that both have just came out of surgery, and that they are doing fine.

Chase closes his eyes, and whispers something under his breath. When the Professor catches up to him, he too is relieved at the good news. A doctor, who informs them that the two injured young men should make a full recovery, now approaches both.

Chase is anxious to see his friends, but the doctor now tells him, "Not today, they need their rest."

CHAPTER 13

Chase and the Professor visit their friends in the hospital every day. A week later as Ethan and Joseph slowly recover from their injuries, the Professor has a meeting with the three young men. With just them in the room, the Professor begins to explain to them, "It is very important that the Shadow Beasts remain unknown. If word was to get out that these creatures actually existed, than a great opportunity to study them in the wild will have been lost."

The three young men nod their heads in agreement, as they remain silent.

"The Shadow Beasts," he continues, "will be hunted and put into a zoo, if they aren't killed first."

Pausing for a moment, he can see that the three young men are very interested in his efforts to save these creatures.

"These remarkable animals are intelligent and caring." He points over at Chase and says, "Just ask Chase, he will tell you."

Chase shakes his head, saying, "They did save my life, and we do need to protect them."

With that said, the Professor asks each of them, "Please do not mention to anyone, what has occurred in the last couple of days."

Without hesitation, they completely agree with the Professor. Now they each take an oath of secrecy not to mention to anyone about the existence of the Shadow Beasts.

As much as these three college students would love to tell their friends about their amazing adventure and discovery, they realize how important it is that all of this be kept a secret.

The weeks pass slowly and the day finally comes, when Ethan and Joseph can leave the hospital.

Waiting out front is Chase, who will drive them home. Ethan, Joseph, and Chase stand next to their car. With Ethan on crutches, his right leg in a cast. Joseph can walk, with the aid of a cane, his right shoulder taped heavily, and a bandage is around his head. The three friends hold each other for a moment.

Joseph tells them, "It is as the Great Spirit showed me."

Thankful to be alive, the three friends get into the car and drive away.

Four years have now passed, and Chase did become a doctor, a veterinarian. He works at an animal hospital, in the city of Eugene, in the state of Oregon. Each summer he takes a vacation and heads north, where he meets his old friend Professor Montgomery. Chase performs a checkup on the Shadow Beasts, and tends to any of their other needs. He always makes sure that he stops at a certain Indian Reservation on his way back, to visit two other old friends.

Ethan had also switched his major since returning to college. He is now an anthropologist, and teaches at the University of Wisconsin in Madison. He also keeps in touch with Professor Montgomery, and his two college friends.

As for Joseph, he is now a Tribal Leader on the Yakama Indian Reservation. Joseph is busy teaching the young ones in his tribe about the ways of their Ancestors, and he proudly wears the bear claw on a necklace around his neck. He has also become a very good storyteller, just like his grandfather.